THE BEASTS

THE
BEASTS

LESLIE GARRETT

CHARLES SCRIBNER'S SONS　　New York

For
Seymour
who is a magician

THE BEASTS

One cold winter sunless morning a group of men stood huddled upon a vacant lot in the downtown section of San Francisco. For the most part they were derelicts: behind them rose long cenotaphs of early-morning buildings, as bleak as they. There were about thirty of them in the city at that time: at night one could see them, in their long overcoats, like bears shuffling from doorway to doorway. But during this period of time those thirty were enlisted there; they were the chosen.

Upright beside each of them were six-foot *papier-mâché* facsimiles of bottles of champagne. Below the neck of each bottle was an oblong eyehole: when they donned them they would look like prisoners peering out from behind their steel cell doors. Across each bottle was the name, in exact replica of the newly advertised original:

JENSEN'S CALIFORNIA CHAMPAGNE
"The Happy Drink"

9

The men would put these on when given their routes for the day, and they would go off inside them over the city.

Now they were waiting. They stood in little groups mostly, except for one. There were some fingerless or limbless as derelicts often are; nearly all drank, not often against the cold, from pint bottles of wine they carried with them. One or two had even slept the night on the lot, huddled around fires, having spent their small pay on wine: these rose eerily from the lot at dawn like scarecrows come suddenly to life. Each slept during that night with his six-foot bottle clutched tightly to him for fear of it being stolen; by morning they were stiffened by cold and were eager to be inside them and about the warming day's activity. They stood hunched over, beating their feet against the cold hard ground, frost issuing from their mouths like cartoon balloons, but wordless.

But one of them was not of any group; he stood off completely from the others. He was a young man; intense; indeed, he seemed possessed, as if the world around him was not a real world; intrusive; and he had to bring himself time and again back to it. There was about him too a curious delicacy of which the others seemed wary.

When a white convertible drove up at last to the edge of the lot, the men came suddenly to life; when the short, stout man slammed out of it and started across the lot toward them, they gathered quickly into one group to await him.

Except for the younger man; he just moved a few feet in their direction with his bottle and stood to the side of them.

The man wore a very large fedora; he too wore a long overcoat, but of camel's hair with wide, pointed lapels.

There was no delay: he was the sort of man one knew would not be likely to waste time when time was money; then he spoke to them.

He told them Jensen's was the *happy* drink; they must *be* happy. He took from the man nearest him his bottle, carefully removed his fedora and handed it to him to hold; then he put on the bottle.

From inside the bottle his voice was sepulchral, but no less emphatic. He told them, This is the Jensen Jig; then he did a curious little dance, just the quick jigging of his feet, the bottle wobbling above him.

A minute later the bottle was back in the derelict's hands, the fedora was replaced and he stood before them again.

He told them then to put on their bottles, and thirty-odd bottles were lifted aloft, as if they had achieved suddenly a life of their own and risen there. Then, one at a time, the men disappeared inside them: heads vanished slowly; torsos and arms; at last only the bottles were standing there, with feet and parts of legs showing beneath.

All except the young man of course: he still stood with that intense preoccupation involved in his other world until a neighbor bottle turned and called to him through his peephole; and then he disappeared too.

At that, the man beat time vigorously with his fur-lined leather gloves. The bottles wobbled aloft; the legs below them did that quick jig, like the exaggerated waddlings of penguins. A few kept at it longer than others; some did fancy steps to show their enthusiasm; but no sooner had they all stopped than the young man, not having moved, and as if just then, minutes later, received the message of what was expected of him, did his dance: it was so quick and mechanical and frantic it seemed almost insane; and just as quickly, it stopped.

The man looked once sharply at the bottle that contained the young man, then clapped his gloves again as a signal for them to go.

Slowly, almost in single-line parade, they moved off the lot, each doing the little dance as he went. At the lot's edge, they diverged and went off over the city on their appointed routes; and the young man was the last of all to go, dancing too.

2

The young man had come to that party on the desolate, beautiful night California coast eager and expectant. At twenty-three, he had thought love at last might await him there—gentle, secure, certain but romantic love that from the first had been a necessary ingredient of his plan for happiness, success; all that was missing really to complete the plan—or at the very least some vague idea of "cultural" intercourse to round out a personality that had been carefully but precariously nurtured. He read all of the best-selling books, both fiction and non-fiction (from the public library in San Francisco), subscribed to *Time* and *Newsweek* (these were arranged in two piles on the end tables in his fifty-dollar-a-month apartment—a dozen of the latest issues at a time for the entertainment of guests over a period of two years; only there had never been a guest)—in short, did all he could to improve himself in that respect; and therefore had accepted the young poet's invitation to the party with eagerness and, he thought with sudden anger and shame, even gratitude.

To find—bohemians; for that is what they surely were. Leotards and beards and dark glasses and dungarees and some sort of jazz on the hi-fi—not at all the subtle, refined people he had expected to meet. He had met the young poet in a bar in San Francisco (he was now in a corner with two bearded men and a girl whose face was painted pure white, even to her ears and throat—like a clown: the poet had disengaged himself from the young man the moment they had arrived at the party); surly, he had thought at first; but he had trained himself always to reserve judgments of people, and even then seldom express them, and they had discussed a few current novels the young man had read, allowing the poet to do most of the talking, nearly all of which was deprecatory; and when the poet had mentioned the party near Bolinas, that he was alone too on that dreary Saturday afternoon because he had missed his ride and it was impossible due to its remoteness to get there any other way than automobile—then the young man, almost shyly, had remarked that he had a car, a Volkswagen, and for the first time the poet had looked at him with interest, even bought a beer after having accepted half a dozen from the young man with just a touch of contempt, as if it were only right that this over-dressed and slightly ludicrous young man should spend some of his easily acquired money on him.

For he was ludicrous; now and then people would stare at him on the streets. He was fairly tall, a bit under six feet, with a body that had been tempered to leanness in the marshland Louisiana country he had come from (he had spent more than a year losing his southern accent by intense study and practice: the first step in his plan); coarse, straw-colored hair. But it was his clothes that caused interest and, frequently, ridicule; for although he tried to emulate the other, successful men in the large insurance company for which he worked, and upon the streets of the Montgomery section where his building was located, those who hurried with initialed Ambassador briefcases through the busy streets—although he tried to be like those bankers and brokers and executives, the impression as yet was more caricature than emulation. His salary did not allow him to invest much money in clothes, and he was forced to seek out cheap imitations that no matter how wonderful and inspiring in the stores with their cunning feeble lighting, when revealed to daylight always looked just that—cheap: no one would mistake a suit of his for a Hart Schaffner & Marx. With his healthy, burned face, his gangling posture, his large, flushed ears that stuck out like ledges, the impression he gave was unrestrained in a world where restraint was tantamount to passion: the ready-made Ivy League suits he bought never fit him; they were usually too small for his awkward build in one place or another. Summer, spring and fall he wore a gray Panama hat with a darker gray broad band that he handled with the utmost delicacy, as if it were alive; and on any morning that gave even the faintest promise of rain, he carried a tightly rolled English-style

15

umbrella with a carved handle. He had had two dismal failures: the first had been the purchase of a homburg that after one day's wear even he had to admit was a bit ostentatious for a seventy-dollar-a-week mailing room clerk, and had put away regretfully; and the second had been the cultivation of a moustache that too had been abandoned after some pointed remarks from one of the executive's secretaries. The moustache had shown signs of wandering sparsely over all of his upper lip, and to his further embarrassment was a color that was an indefinite mixture of red and blond.

So now he was there—with the bohemians. He stood alone holding a can of beer, his eyes moving over the three large rooms he could see—the dining-room where he stood, with a big table, wicker chairs and a windowseat stretching the length of the entire room, the large windows reminiscent of the captain's cabin in an Errol Flynn pirate's galleon: through them, in moonlight, the lawn was thick with weeds and stunted trees, some dead, their long, bent branches as if clawing the earth and the ink-black sky. Beyond the proper yard of the house, the earth dipped sharply onto a bright belt of beach; beyond that the ocean was murmurous with white curls of breakers, the full, bright moon sunk down and half hidden like a wafer dunked in some mammoth cup; it was magnificent. And the quite ordinary kitchen with its clattering old square refrigerator and sink and the young poet and the bearded men and the girl with the white-painted face; the big, sparsely furnished front room, where most of the people were, about twenty all told, talking in groups or seated upon the floor against the walls. One young man held a long cigarette holder extended before him as if he were haughtily unfamiliar with it. A not unattractive girl in dirty dungarees and black turtleneck sweater sat brooding by herself on the floor in a corner staring down between her legs at sockless feet and a pair of torn white sneakers. Now and then she sighed to herself; her shoulders heaved misery and hopelessness beneath the cropped black hair that barely covered her ears. Now and then too the girl looked up with harrowing eyes at a group the center of which seemed to be a huge Negro in blue, baggy suit, shoestring tie and a white shirt. It was not just that the Negro was large; he was monstrous. He was perhaps just a bit under seven feet; a giant in fact; proportionately broad, with large ham-like hands that had been used obviously for years in toil; but there was something about the eyes, the face, that proclaimed a hate-filled but flaccid nature seeking completion. The eyes were very small; but fierce and strange in that broad, huge face. The Negro was very drunk, and the young man stared at him for a long time: around the Negro's head was a towel wound into a turban.

With an effort, the young man turned away from the Negro. It was, in fact, with a little jerking movement of which he was not aware. These movements were common to him; as if incomplete himself; as if moving in an alien body.

It was hot in the room; his collar pinched; and he

turned to look out of the window again when he saw his reflection in it: in one hand was the can of beer, and in the other, carefully cradled atop his arm, as in some eighteen nineties' daguerreotype, was the precious Panama hat: he looked as if he were awaiting a formal ceremony or processional.

He looked at the girl again. What was unfortunately a very active imagination, a quality of mind that was the greatest possible detriment to his ambitions, went to work: she was alone; she was lonely; the world had hurt her. Immediately he manufactured pity for her, and therefore for himself. He took his hat and placed it atop a tall, empty china closet where it was out of danger of being crushed, adjusted his shirt cuffs and his thin tie knotted to the size of a rosebud, and, forcing a smile and a bit of *savoir-faire* (he had captured that phrase with particular hunger, noting it carefully, with its translation, in a little notebook he kept with him at all times for such purposes), entered the front room and stood beside the girl, who was seated staring intently down into her lap.

He tried to appear casual: "Well, miss, you look a tiny bit lonely."

The girl looked up: close to her now, he saw with a shock her wide, insane eyes. "What?"

"What I mean is, excuse me, I don't know nobody here."

He stiffened at his error in grammar; hoped she had not noticed it: in spite of his painful attempts at sophistication, he was always miserable, uncertain of himself, at parties.

To ease the panic, he brought himself to stare at her face. It was a face that was almost beautiful, with the intense, twisted monomania of the ravaged child; wistful and onerously sad. The eyes looked up at him, the strangest, most frightening eyes he had ever seen, vacant and staring, with the whites dominant and expressionless, like a doll's, or a madwoman's, and giving the impression she was not seeing him at all but some vision within herself.

"I'll tell you because you do not look cruel, this is going to be a strange night," she said. "I can feel it."

He coughed discreetly into his fist. "Really? How do you know?"

She waved her hand at the room. "I can feel it. Vibrations. I can feel them in you too."

"Vibrations?" The laugh came out suddenly; shrill and girlishly high; so that then a few faces turned to him; then away with disinterest. The laugh, long practiced before mirrors, was intended to be a blending of sardonic incredulity and amusement; instead it had issued cracked and like a crow's cawing.

In actual panic now, he turned and hurried off.

A moment later she was standing next to him by the window. She was small: the top of her head came only to his chest. She looked up at him suddenly severe: "Why did you run off? People are always running off from me." She said it angrily.

"I'm sorry," he said. "I don't feel well." He decided: she was quite pretty. But she wore no makeup of any kind; her clothes looked as if she had picked them up off the streets, and her face and hands and feet . . . . :

he knew with a shudder she had not bathed in weeks, and he touched his own face and clothes in a reflex of assurance: the cuffs of his freshly laundered shirt were satisfyingly stiff with starch beneath his fingers.

The poet and the girl with the painted face left their group and walked slowly, almost in rhythm, into one of the two bedrooms, closing the door. The young man watched them and then turned away with an expression of disgust that he saw reflected in the window. He did not approve of promiscuity; love was noble, creative. "I don't want to sound like a . . . a square," he said, "but I don't approve of that sort of thing."

"What sort of thing?" The girl had been bent over and intensely absorbed in picking still more holes in her sneakers; she had not seen the poet and the girl; perhaps did not see much of anything, he thought; but he softened the thought.

He waved his hand in the direction of the secreted lovers in an hysterical gesture that even he did not understand.

But she only said "Oh" in a disinterested way and stood up then, biting the skin reflectively from around her thumbnail. And then she said the most unexpected thing: "I've only had relations with one person here."

He did not comment. He looked nervously again at his reflection in the window, but she continued:

"Him."

She was pointing: he looked. He was confused for a moment and did not understand, and then he understood: *the Negro*. His jaw dropped suddenly before he could control himself, and he felt the perspiration starting upon his forehead. She seemed to brood over this for a moment, stooped over slightly and still chewing the skin from her thumbnail with little grimaces now and then. "He raped me. You see, that's how it really happened; he raped me. I pity him for that."

"My God! Did you call the police?"

"No. The Father-God will punish him," she said.

She looked over broodingly at the Negro, who stood mammoth above the other men in the room. Then she said, not so much to him as to herself, or the air, "He calls himself the Prophet."

"Of what?" he asked.

"Everyone's a prophet of one thing or another," she said.

She bit her lip, still looking speculatively at the Negro, then shook her head vigorously, as if ridding herself of some vision, and looked up fiercely at him.

That was how it started.

Suddenly the entire night changed: the moon, the stars, the ocean. He was just a little drunk by the time they left the house; she was more drunk than he, although she had only a few glasses of wine, and as they passed the crowded kitchen out of the house, she walked in the strangest way—almost stooped over, her head twisted away from people to one side, as if she were a small quarterback charging blindly through a line—and he noticed she did not speak to anyone and remembered that few people had spoken to her

21

during all of the evening; yet he was certain she was known by all of the others.

The entire night changed for him then; strangely. There before them was the huge moon, the bright stars, the night; there was the white beach and the sand-hillocks, the bowls of shadows like craters, the tumbling breakers along the damp and windy shore; and behind them the house itself between two trees that bent over it, as if confiding unhurried and conspirate an immemorial secret—but alive within with lights and laughter and music. Now and then someone would come onto the porch in a blaze of light, from where they stood on the beach like tiny actors strolled onto a pantomime stage: it was, to the young man as he walked drunkenly with the girl, vibrant, profound and almost unendurably poetic. And now here was he, in all that moonbright, vast and passionate night, walking with this strange, moody girl.

They had not spoken much, had not exchanged more than a dozen sentences, and she walked beside him silent and brooding; and yet he could feel the change, the chemistry of love and strangeness. It was not in him to question it, to wonder if perhaps it was not more circumstance and convenience and an identification through need; his was a passionate nature that until then had been stifled; but now it had changed: it was beautiful and there was poetry in the night.

She was walking barefoot now, carrying her almost shredded sneakers, her toes digging into the sand as they walked; and in his sudden assent to passion, he reached down and removed his own shoes and socks.

They stood finally on a little hillock overlooking the ocean. The sand was cool beneath his feet, and he stretched up on his toes, his arms outspread as if to embrace the moon. Then he looked at the girl, and suddenly he felt sad, almost tearful. He thought of her life, and he was certain it was cruel and unremitting misery, and instead of embracing the moon he turned with his arms still outstretched, and embraced her.

For a moment he was certain he would hold her without passion, as if he could placate with that embrace all of her misery and loneliness; but before he could, the embrace tightened as he felt her small, tensed body pressed against him; and it was no longer compassion he felt.

But he had placed himself awkwardly; they were off balance on the hillock, their legs entwined; and as he leaned forward he lost his footing and toppled down onto the sand, bringing her with him.

There was no mirth about it: she was silent, almost pensive, and he was ecstatic; but he did not laugh.

They righted themselves and sat on the hillock overlooking the ocean: shattered moonlight flashed— long, silver fish of light darting and rocking there upon slow black bellies of water. She sat hunched over, her legs drawn up and her chin upon her crossed arms, peering out. He looked out at the moon again, the ocean, the sky. He too was still, almost brooding watching her, and cautiously he asked the question: "About what happened, what that Negro did . . ."

She looked up sharply then, perhaps for the first time in minutes aware of him. "What?"

"About the Negro," he said slowly "—what he did to you."

"I don't want to talk about it now," she said. "If you're really not cruel, you won't ask me to talk about it."

"Of course," he said. "It must have been terrible."

"I've been trying to decide whether I can trust you," she said.

"You can trust me."

"I don't know. I've trusted so many people. I don't believe in trust any more. Only the Father-God."

"I think I love you," he said.

Her face hardened, and for a moment he thought she was going to say something contemptuous, scornful, but she didn't. He watched, again in panic, as she reached down and unzipped her dungarees and soundlessly discarded them; as she flung aside her sneakers, her sweater and brassiere. A moment later they lay side by side, he hastily trying to discard his clothes unseen as she clung to him. Finally they were both naked under the bright moonlight. He thought for a moment he should tell her he loved her, but he didn't.

His name was Farley Grimm, and after that night he did not see the girl again for nearly a month. The

24

morning after the party, awakening hungover and sick
with that pervasive suffering that is the strayed moral-
ist's after intoxication—that morning he sat shaking
on the side of his bed in his tidy apartment and decided positively he would not see her again. He knew
her name—Lenore—and her address, but he swore he
would not see her or communicate with her. He decided he had taken advantage of her, that in her un-
happiness and madness (he could not rid himself of
that thought: driving back to the city that night, she
had sat slumped down nearly flat in the seat, as if trying
to hide there, had not said one word to him during all
of the long ride, had ignored his attempts at conversation, and had finally, when he had stopped before the
old building in the North Beach section where she
lived, slammed out of the car and with that strange,
hunched-over and heavy walk of hers disappeared into
the building without so much as a word) she had
given herself to him out of need rather than desire,
that he had sensed this but nevertheless had "enjoyed"
her, and therefore had been morally irresponsible.
There was also the fact that she was strange, that she
was emotionally unpredictable, that she wore those
old, dirty clothes, or others, he was sure, equally disreputable, that she wore no makeup of any kind . . .
that, in short, she was as far from his ideal of a mate
as he could imagine.

So it was decided. He went back to his job, his
routine. He went each day to his office; in the evenings
he prepared spare, planned meals in the small kitchen

of his apartment, doing the dishes carefully and with sensual pleasure immediately after; then he would sit in his parlor dutifully reading the latest magazines or books. Several times a week he would go to a movie or the library in the evenings, and on Saturday mornings he would do his weekly shopping at the Piggly Wiggly Market; and on Saturday afternoons clean the tiny apartment and take his weekly laundry to the laundromat. Saturday nights he would dress in his best clothes and stroll down Market Street or go to one of three cocktail lounges where there were thick carpets and piano players and in the men's rooms blue lights and deodorants. He would sit stiffly at the bar on the tall stool with his hat placed carefully on another stool beside him and drink beer. To each of the three bartenders he was known as the boy who was careful never to let his shirt cuffs touch the bar as he lifted his sixty-cent bottles of beer.

Once, however, he got a little drunk on his Saturday night. He walked unsteadily up Market Street, the lights of that busy downtown street almost blue: a mist of blue light. That night when he went home he sat fully dressed, even to hat, on the very edge of the sofa in his quiet apartment: if anyone had seen him they would have thought him a stranger there carefully awaiting the real occupant of the apartment. The sofa was of a coarse material, with flowers and static birds embossed upon it, and a severe, straight back. Finally he stumbled to bed and, consciously, evoked even more clearly the image that had been haunting him all that night: the girl and the Negro. Finally he gave himself up to it completely with a little moan in the darkness.

It was the next night that he went to see the girl again.

He sat in the living room upon a sofa so torn and disreputable it looked as if it had been dragged in off the streets: white stuffing popped out of it from a dozen tears. The girl sat across from him on the only other furnishing in the room—a bare mattress—cross-legged and barefooted and hunched over tensely. He cleared his throat.

"I've been meaning to call," he said, and then they both were silent.

She picked at her toes with a furious concentration, as if she were counting them, her face pressed close over them.

Finally he steadied himself, went over and sat down next to her upon the mattress. Paint-smeared rags were scattered over the length of the room, and beside the only window was an empty easel, and around this upon the floor rags too and about six jars and glasses: from the neck of one protruded a thick assortment of brushes hardened from disuse; the others contained liquids colored by the droppings of paints, like some weird aquarium within which sea-creatures billowed among wisps of strange plants.

"I've been meaning to call, Lenore," he said again, and, trembling, reached suddenly for her and brought her down roughly beside him upon the mattress.

They made love there: a large, unshaded 200-watt bulb blazed from the ceiling (all of the overhead bulbs in the apartment were fierce, and unshaded, and, as he was to learn later, burned day and night, even when she was out), and when it was over Farley lay back staring up at it. She lay next to him upon her back, her eyes closed and her hands at her sides shut tightly into fists. She had not wanted to; and now she lay rigid and walled off from him. He wanted to conciliate her, and so he told her the words she did not want to hear: "I love you," he said, not knowing that it was for himself a sort of redemption, an offering, an oblation: wholly unsatisfactory in that it intensified the guilt he had intended to alleviate.

At the moment, the actual moment of sexual contact, he had been horrified: she had shaved herself. At that moment the madness of it seized him; at the first touch he had drawn back in panic: there were only the coarse, emergent bristles, like a man's day-old unshaven face.

Later he told himself he had not questioned her then out of delicacy, but now, lying beside her upon the bare mattress, he extracted a cigarette from his coat upon the floor beside him, lit it and finally asked the question:

"Why did you shave yourself?"

"What?" She opened her eyes; suddenly, he thought, she almost uncoiled beside him in a change of mood that seemed to be without any gradations whatsoever.

"You shaved yourself there," he said. "Why?"

"Oh." She leaned over, took the cigarette from his fingers. For a moment it appeared she was about to take a puff, but instead she lowered it before it reached her lips and ground it out on the floor at their heads.

"It's something the Father-God told me to do," she said. "When He tells me to do something, I do it. He's the only one I can trust." Then: "Once, when I was sixteen, I was in a sanitarium; He told me to shave off all of my hair then too—my head, my eyebrows, my armpits and there. He hasn't told me to do that for a long time, though."

Later, they moved into the bedroom. There, another bright bulb blazed from the ceiling over soiled, scattered clothes, another bare mattress without even a pillow, an orange crate jammed full with rags and an assortment of clothes of many fashions and decades (he was to learn later that compassionate persons, both friends and strangers, stirred to charity, were forever giving gifts of clothes to her, which she accepted silently, often lugging large bundles for blocks to her apartment and shoving them finally away in crates and corners and wearing few of them), the orange crate upended and disgorging clothes and rags. There, finally, tentatively, he reached out and explored that disquieting stubble: accepted it finally with a sigh of relief, even excitement when they again made love.

They were a strange pair. They became lovers then, and he went nearly each night to her apartment where they made love often beneath the blazing lights. He

was always dressed—suit, starched white shirt, tie—
and even during the first month he would sit always
straight and proper upon the collapsed and gutted
couch, legs lined carefully before him and the inevit-
able Panama hat balanced carefully upon his knees:
the Gentleman Caller.

And she: now it was no longer the dungarees and
old sweater, but a red smock she had discovered in a
trash can on some midnight wandering: it was several
sizes too large for her, and to Farley bore an uncomfortable resemblance to a maternity dress (The child
seeking child? he thought). When she was in one of
her brooding moods she could sit on the floor in a corner, or upon the mattress, and, drawing in her arms and
legs and face, nearly disappear into it for hours at a
time—much like a turtle gone into its shell, and only
now and then looking out morosely from behind the
wide collar. For the first week she wore it she would not
take it off at all, not even when they made love, and at
first he felt as if she were some shell-like animal peering up at him with dark, mistrustful eyes. Once he
looked down and there was no face at all beneath him,
only that collar within which she had chosen even at
that moment to hide. Shocked then, it had later excited him; and the next night, on his way to her, he
had trembled at the thought of making love to her
again like that, and had run the last three blocks to
the house.

But he was the Gentleman Caller: he brought her
candy, flowers, presents. The candy was always eaten

quickly by her; the flowers shrivelled in slow spasms within jars aqueous with paints and chemicals; and the presents opened, inspected and seldom seen again (put away in the crates with the discarded clothes, he assumed).

He was the Gentleman Caller: he took her to movies, for walks, to restaurants. He was aware of the stares of strangers (they each had about them an aura of unreality, as if just walked from a movie set), the grotesqueness of their pairing; but there was a sort of love there, a need generated by his years of loneliness, of self-imposed discipline; and in his apartment later he would dream of a life with her—he secure in his position of prominence in that great company, she the proper, charming wife of the executive. Then, there were no erotic images in his dreams of her. One night he asked himself the question directly: "Why not?" There was certainly, to him, then no reason why not. There were moments when she was just that—gay, free of the brooding and suspicions, and when she might possibly have assumed the role.

He was often full of a quiet tenderness toward her after they had made love; and that night too he allowed himself to remember what she had told him on the first night—about the Negro—and tenderness and a desire to comfort and protect her rose in him at the thought of the horror of her life.

He felt proud that night, noble; but the next morning the feeling was gone, and during all of that day the image persisted: the girl and the Negro. He could not rid himself of it; it created in him a great, swelling passion such as he had never known: there was warmth in it too, an illicit, he knew, but hungry sensuousness that seemed to burst the edges of that other, erected, self; and that night he did not go to her, but sat in a bar getting drunk and watching the men and women. And at midnight, really drunk for the first time in his life, forsaking the ordered gentility of the cocktail lounges, roaming the streets and bars seeking those phantom lovers, the black man and the white woman; finding them at last in a bar in the Tenderloin; finding too a great, leaping release in the smelling toilet, leaning trembling after with his back to the door of the latchless cubicle.

They were a strange pair. He invited her for dinner at his apartment. It was the fourth month's anniversary of their meeting, and he was excited by the prospect of it. Not only was she the first guest he had ever had in the apartment, but there was something "solid," socially respectable about it; it was as if she were his fiancée.

He spent days planning and preparing for the dinner: there was to be cornish hen, asparagus tips, frozen strawberries for dessert. He consulted one of the secretaries at the office, and chose vermouth cocktails and a bottle of chablis for the meal; he even bought flowers and a glass candelabrum in the shape of two swans' heads rising from a single thin wavering body for the center of the table: it had cost four dollars in a musty old shop on Ellis Street, and he was certain it possessed artistic merits that would impress her favorably. The owner of the shop, a middle-aged woman with enormous shoulders, had viewed him with undisguised contempt during the entire transaction.

She came at seven, came silent and loping through the rooms like some feral creature, a lame deer perhaps in that frightened, clumsy gait. Not a word spoken between them at first, and standing at the doorway of each room as if inspecting, sniffing, uncertain of welcome and not wanting to intrude uninvited upon any private place. She was always like that: cautious and silent in unaccustomed places, secure against harm and abuse only among known places, trusted people.

The apartment had been thoroughly cleaned: there was not an article out of place, not a sign of dust or use: the rooms were like the re-assembled rooms of kings and queens in museums—unused—with even the aura now of the velvet rope before each room to restrain her. He followed silently behind her, pleased and a little proud, then excused himself on the threshold of the bedroom with what might have been a bow, and went to make the vermouth cocktails. She turned and loped back into the living room, her head still lowered and thrust a little to one side as if expecting a blow, and sat down on the coarse, severe couch with fat dull-blue birds winging around her upon the harsh material.

She heard him humming in the kitchen in a solemn, husky voice: *la donna è mobile*.

He returned with the cocktails upon a metal tray:

painted red, birds soared and nested there too in flatulent obesity. A single cube of ice tinkled in each wide blue-frosted glass, the gilt initials FG in Roman script emitting distinct frosty pearls. He sat down at the opposite end of the couch from her and reflectively sniffed the vermouth.

She wore the red smock even then. A charm bracelet he had given her, the only jewelry he had ever seen her wear, jangled upon her wrist beyond the sleeve of the smock. She did not touch her drink, but when he had finished his he went into the kitchen and made another for himself. He drank that there and fixed another; then he saw his hands were trembling.

They ate at a card table in the living room. Dexterously, with practiced precision, he sliced the meat for them, filling her plate; on his he put one slice. This act was particularly pleasurable for him; the set he used was bone-handle, monogrammed too, and the knife always sharpened by him to a razor-fineness. Now, slicing the last piece, he gave an extra flourish of the knife, both to reveal its quality and demonstrate further his skill.

By then it was dark and he had lit the candles and they ate by candlelight. Although he had poured her a glass, she did not touch the wine. She ate the food ravenously, as if she had not eaten for days, trembling over it.

He was touched; it had not occurred to him before that she might often go hungry. If she had been starving, he knew she would not mention it to him. He thought she would waste away and die before his eyes of hunger before she would complain: suffering was that natural to her, and even her periods of bitterness were never expressed in words. He reached over and touched her hand. "Lenore, I want to take care of you."

She looked up, startled. "How?"

"I would like us to be together—always."

She shrugged and went back to her plate. "If you want," she said.

It was settled for him: he would move in with her.

Before the dinner was over he had finished nearly all of the bottle of wine; he was drunk. They sat on the sofa together and he started to make love to her.

"I want to take care of you," he said. "I want to love you."

"What is love?" she said.

That night they made love in his bedroom, upon sheets for the first time.

She insisted that the lights stay on, and he that she wear the smock.

3

He called himself the Prophet: she told him that.
And more.

She had come from the Allegheny country of Penn-
sylvania at seventeen, limping and ragged and swollen-
footed from some midnight harried journey: emerged
from rocks and streaked city pavements and endless
desert; a room where a tin basin clattered, a bed
screeched: midnight and endless until the final
brindled western sun. Leaving behind some young
mad slender husband of virgin nights; some (by turns)
vicious, tender madboy with hands like a girl's (he had
decided he was a businessman then: she remembered
him adjusting the new homburg in the car mirror,
the elk's tooth and watchfob upon his tightly buttoned
vest), who had tormented to the last the aunt who
raised him by what she came to term his "rapacious
sensitivity." Came finally then to that westernmost
city through all of the gray days, catatonic nearly, madness veiled, in which upon parkbenches in blistering
noons transfigured old men seemed scabrous, sedentary
beasts from whom she hid in the sudden impacted

36

room, trembling upon the floor before the bed: some man slept there, dark and hairy, some brief and brutal lover, unnamed. It was a long journey, unremembered; shorn and shaven, hairless herself, she had fled that wedded nightmare, as she had fled the insular nightmare, that place of gray long corridors, murmurings and false felicity, with that boy whose madness was not even a complement to her own (she remembered later: there was finally no job to go to and that homburg fitted grotesquely upon a shaved head): she was wedded to madness then in gleaming rooms, before his posed reflection in a dozen tinted mirrors, his hairless, passionless embrace at night: fleeing this, they had come in what might have been one night or one year conjoined in final madness, that last fearful copulation all hairless and powdered that had evolved from what they must once have thought of as salvation.

That was over.

And so she came then finally to the city of hills, that westernmost city. To the North Beach section of that white city, where ancient Italians sat in proud lineage before tired bohemians: the saint of Assisi brooded ponderous above relics of human desire, but there was no wedding of spirit or flesh, no misbegotten of mind or heart in all of the last half of one century and the first half of the next; nor was there likely to be any in centuries to come.

A middle-aged Lesbian, a sculptress, took her in first. Beyond suspirant folds of Japanese kimonos her flesh was furrowed and brown as rotting fruit; brittle twigs of fingers waved ten perfect scarlet crescent moons below the cumbersome wings of sleeves: the dark bird fluttered, tumbling toward unsuccessful flight through all of those five gleaming Spartan rooms, that desiccate body desireless, whether through wisdom or lack of it she never knew. But never bothered, left with paints and paper upon a marble floor: she had painted for the first time then under the critical eye of the big woman.

Painted birds. Birds and small animals like knobs of fur with black, sad, frightened eyes. Birds scrofulous in grotesque, horny, humanfooted ploddings through tangled forests.

And strange too all of those months, the times of the bright metallic light, sunlight upon those marble floors, pounded like broken clubs upon bare tables and puffed beasts of chairs: in the foyer a bronze nymphet posed bright and balletic upon glistening rocks in a small fountain: colored lights played and revolved below trickling water, expanding and traveling like swift silent fish.

Until one day the big woman was gone, and she was alone in the bright, gleaming rooms. She could stay on there for the rest of the month, and she wandered from room to room. Most of the furniture was covered then with sheets, and she loped like a small, aimless animal in some dead glacial land from soundless room to soundless room. There was a hundred dollar bill in an envelope left there for her by the big woman; she shoved it into the back pocket of her dungarees; and two weeks later a postcard came from Bern, Switzerland, showing a Swiss chalet with great snowcovered mountains behind and a young, redfaced, grinning man on skis before the chalet: his face and hands were leathery; red; and his curly hair was bleached blond by sun, and that grinning, boyish face proclaimed youth and certitude and vitality to all the world. The message was only two words, the last one of which was the woman's name: "LOVE, Thorn."

Love: even the lights were extinguished in that fountain, the bronze nymphet poised as if in surprised nakedness.

That brought her into the world of the people of the Beach. She had now and then sat in those bars and coffeehouses with the big woman, both strangers really, alien in that penumbral world, and she voiceless —shadow, companion: she had sat slouched over the tables, staring glumly into her glass or cup, dwarfed by the big woman and finding in that a sort of sanctuary. No one had ever spoken to her, and she did not even know their faces.

And so she came into that world, that world of erected ghosts and the seared dreams, all ashridden and turned in upon themselves: contorted. It did not matter; for it was not expedience, or even choice, but because it was simply there, the nearest, and it was like stepping through darkness from one dimly lighted stage to the next.

And the next; endlessly perhaps before each new sensed but faceless crowd.

She sat in the bars, the coffeehouses. She never

bought anything. The hundred dollars was almost forgotten; it lay crumpled in her pocket, and when once she did take it out, examining it curiously in her hunger with the idea of purchasing a meal—then the one quick thought of the difficulty in using so large a bill for any small purchase had defeated her, frightened her by the infinite possibilities of involvement, and she had hastily replaced it, erased it from memory as some perversely guarded and mnemonic token of another life. But she did not have to use the bill, for always there seemed someone eventually to buy the meal, the cup of coffee, the occasional glass of wine. As for shelter, she could always sleep on a bench in the back of a bar; or upon the floor or a couch in some couple's flat (she did not need much sleep, and she would sneak off, at dawn, silent, stealthy, rather than disturb her benefactors, or intrude herself upon their daylight hours: not a morsel of food or a single possession was ever taken), by day roaming the streets and the parks until it was time to return again to those bars and coffeehouses.

She was accorded a kind of patronage among them: men were roused to forgotten protective manhood by the sight of her; and women, a sort of maternal righteousness at any affront to her. She was the Child to all, the symbol perhaps of that very brief flown innocence and passivity that they could not have acknowledged wanting back in any other way.

There was love, of course, of a sort: once, with a young poet, in a large room upon a cushioned couch.

The doors opened upon hinges of cobwebs, and spider-webs upon each corner of the beamed and barn-like ceiling. Books lined all the walls, and in red paint above the doorway, emphatic as lightning, the message, ALL IS LOVE. That night incense burned in a cracked cup upon the mantel, and below it, the only light, the pulsing, flushed face of a gasheater that below the quivering spiral of scented smoke took on the aspect of a grinning unicorn's head. He had a beard and long uncut fingernails like talons, and during the moment of passion, buried, drowning, lost beneath him, sunk in that ocean of cushions that smelled of must and flesh and spent passion, then he raked her flesh—twice, deliberately—with those sharp nails, holding her squirming, struggling body fast beneath him, like some passionless murderer forcing his victim beneath water. Later, he had leaped hairy and drooping from the couch and made tea. He sat beside her on the couch as they drank, his shrivelled sac and phallus burrowing between the cushions. She could feel the torn flesh of her back and she lay shivering in the damp and musty room, and when again he came it was carrying a kitchen plate upon which burned two dozen candles upon a scaly, varicolored mound of wax, the drippings from perhaps a hundred other candles; came solemnly from out of the darkness of the kitchen as if bearing a sacrament and placed it upon a table at her feet: the candles pulsed upon their shapeless mound; and again he mounted the couch, his body thick with patches of black hair even upon his shoulders and neck, his erected phallus probing; and then descended. . . . Later they sat out in his patio, he still naked and she clothed then. He smoked cigarette after cigarette, seated upon the brick steps, and talked to her of love: scornfully, impatiently, as if she were a dull and unworthy disciple he had for want of someone better condescended to instruct—she hunched over as usual in the lush night. There was moonlight; vines and wildflowers grew in the ravaged jungle that was his patio; lizards skittered unseen through trembling tunnels of grass; a figtree had dropped its bursted fruit; and a marble slab, a tombstone, against one wall like the single stone petal of a giant flower: here he talked of love, telling her that love was the temporal, the immediate, a ritual the object of which was the confiscation of all knowledge. He told her many things, but she hardly listened. Behind them, through the filmy and dirt-encrusted window, that mound of candles burned dull and wavering in the darkened room like some distant fiery polydactyl monster burning the night; and when she returned the following afternoon (shyly, quietly, through the gate, hunched over as she approached across the crackling path of dead leaves and twigs in the warm sunlight) he was again seated upon the steps of the patio, and she approached in silence, her face to the ground and hardly looking at them; for now there was another person seated upon those steps with him, a woman, and they watched her approach in silent, conspirate amusement. The woman was tall and slender, and her fingers and nails were as long and as sharp as the poet's, and from one hand protruded poised as if in tired benediction a long black cigarette holder. Her plucked eyebrows were hairthin, like minute arched snakes above tired eyes. . . . She did not need to be told; with one quick furtive glance she knew, and before she had even approached them turned and loped (only more bent over now, so that she appeared deformed) before their amused gaze from the sunbright place.

That was one.

And one lover, one brief lover, was tender. He was a boy of eighteen, as homeless as she. He was thin to the point of emaciation, and penniless, and all during that winter month he wore the same large, ragged overcoat buttoned always to the collar, and when they were for the first time about to make love she saw the reason: he did not own a shirt. He never once smiled; his hair grew down over his collar, and although he never had money for food, he was constantly drunk: with sardonic, mirthless humor he told her he had not been sober a day since he was fourteen, and he ran errands in the bars and coffeehouses for nickels and dimes and slept with a series of homosexuals for money and wine. He was handsome and tall and full of bitterness and hatred for the world, and because he could not love her he was kind to her; and because he was poor (and she did not think of the hundred dollar bill; she had not thought of it for months) they spent their first night sitting up in parks and a bus

43

station; and the second night, and every night for all of that month, they spent together upon couches and floors in the rooms and apartments of acquaintances. He was tender. They sat all day and most of the night in those bars then, she almost never speaking, silent companion, shadow to him as she had been to the big woman, and he drinking and speaking to others in that unvaried, bitter, mirthless tone of his, his dark, unshaven face older by decades than his eighteen years: she knew that he was lost—the tired, the nearly vanquished, the comfortless seeker after final despair: he had closed in upon himself like a dark nightflower.

But tender; for if there was love in him he bore it for her during those brief days; sadly, without smile or word, even with what certainly was bitterness, he offered it to her—thrust it, for it was as if some quick phantom bird of light, some brightwinged bird of light, a gift of light, had descended—and was gone: she was aware of its going during the moment of acceptance; and had known always that that was how it would be.

But tender: he gave her a goldfish, strangely, a single goldfish, in a glass jar as his only present. She never knew where he had gotten it (he seldom spoke directly to her, but as if she were the unseen and impersonal object of his desperate thoughts), but after that, wherever they were, upon the street, in one of the bars, in someone's home, there too was the goldfish. A home, a sanctification, the starburnt symbol of their brief grace, their belated felicity (he knew, and refused to know: too finally, certainly, grimly, determinedly seared; she waiting). It was a strange and perhaps beautiful sight to see: she came like a sad comic ballerina, hunched over and intense upon each street balancing the jar and the fish: with her strange walk the jar would sway from side to side, water splashing over her, the bright fish as if balancing perplexed upon an invisible trapeze. Or at a bar, refilling the water, or cleaning it, or feeding the fish, or just sitting at a table with it before her, watching it intently, her face pressed close to the jar as if in secret communication with it: it took less than a week for the fish to die.

But there was no sadness; it was hardly remarked upon; and when at last the boy noticed that it was dead he spoke directly to her for one of the few times: "Get rid of it," he told her, and when later he saw that she had not gotten rid of it, that she even hugged it now obstinately to her, he did not insist. So that after that it was the dead goldfish she carried, not out of perversity, or insanity, but because it was some part of her life she was not yet willing to relinquish. But it did not matter: two days later the boy was gone. She believed someone, a man, had taken him away; there were several who had asked him during that month, and it was not unexpected: he could not endure happiness any more than most men can endure sorrow.

Suddenly there was the Prophet. He appeared one day alone, and the following day he was the center of all attention, and the next day he wore a twenty-dollar western shirt one of the women had given him, and the next day he was living with a young blonde woman who made a desultory living as a whore: when he arrived he had not had a penny and had worked for an hour as a dishwasher for a meal; now he sat disdainfully with his own bottle of scotch at the bar.

The Prophet: more caricature than prophet, bizarre and perhaps mad too; cunning surely, festering with hatred—yet the intensity of that caricature, the audacity that inspired him to couple it with his grotesque hugeness, compelling beyond mere inventiveness: his power was always shortlived, his conquests brief; the novelty soon wore off and he moved from city to city. He had a sort of genius: he called up briefly the secret admiration in all of us for evil made comfortable to face.

He did not believe in himself; there was no doubt about that: as if merely the idea of being a prophet were enough; *entrée*, he had discovered; and incapable, or it never occurring to him, of defining it further.

In his late-thirties, his was a ravaged face, wasted and alcoholic: it was a face in which hatred had been tempered with cunning.

There was something insane about him too; for he wore a plain white bathtowel wound into a turban upon his head; and in the center of the turban and fastened to it with a safety-pin a rhinestone brooch obviously from the counter of a five-and-dime.

He professed an intimate knowledge of the Black

Mass, however, and this plus a collection of pornographic films (in several of which he was the principal actor and displayed an extraordinary physical attribute that fitted him admirably for the part) and a ready and seemingly inexhaustible supply of marijuana—these brought him immediate acceptance among them.

Hatred, violence leaped from him: many feared him instinctively as a man capable of the greatest violence without regard for consequences. Although no conversation with him was ever of any consequence, as one resident expressed it, *any* conversation with him was like walking barefoot upon eggshells.

To the girl he was another of the shadows. She wandered then, as she had done before, from place to place; and once she was at a party where he was showing the pornographic films on someone's projector; and she had wandered briefly from room to room. All of the other rooms had been dark, bluelighted, and she had hurried through them glowering in the unfriendly darkness. Stooped over, face to the floor as usual, she had heard only dimly the soft humming of the machine, been but vaguely aware as she entered of its pulsing, mothfluttering tracery of light.

Until she looked up startled and, suddenly blinded by light, stared into the throbbing eye of it. She had stood there a full five seconds, startled, voices calling angrily to her from that bodiless darkness, parts of faces and hands like birds bobbing and soaring upon the spear of light. She had stood dazed, uncomprehending for a moment among shouts and imprecations,

47

caught in the sudden blaze between machine and screen, the broken and distorted images fluttering jerkily upon her face and arms and chest. Someone pushed her then, and she had stumbled through darkness toward the door and found her way out of the house.

The Prophet himself came down later to console her. He and the woman (she had inch-long fingernails painted a deep purple, and bracelets jangled and glinted from each wrist, and a fat, bloated face like a baby's peered gloomily below large picture hats) sought her out in one of the bars later. They sat across from one another at a table. The woman's pudgy red hand covered the Negro's at the table; the girl could see coarse red hairs upon it, the hand heavily freckled and the hairs sprouting, minuscule, from the centers of freckles. When she finally looked, the squat woman was leaning forward upon her elbows looking directly at her; and her face too was covered with hundreds of freckles upon the pink skin.

With a disdainful flourish, the Prophet ordered a bottle of scotch for himself, a beer for the woman and a soda for the girl.

He raised his hand above his head, holding it there a moment until some of the people in the bar had stopped talking and turned to him; then he said, quite drunkenly,

"You can all kiss my black ass."

"What do you want?" the girl asked. "I don't have much time."

The Prophet seemed surprised at the question; his face suddenly became lined, almost weary with disappointment.

"We just want to love you," he sighed.

The woman nodded her agreement. From her large picture hat dozens of tiny birds dangled upon wires; now they swayed in slow agitation.

"You see," the Prophet began slowly, his face suddenly tense with concentration, as if he were about to recite a speech he had long before prepared but was never certain of remembering, "when God made man He made him to love *His* image. We got to get God back into our lovin'; we got to love *Him*; otherwise we corrupted. You love me and you *got* to love God; cause *I'm* His fiery angel."

He stopped and drank another glass of scotch, his fifth. His eyes were abnormally close together, separated only by a thin, hawk-like nose. He seemed to become suddenly gloomy and stared into his glass for a long time.

"You ever prayed?" he asked at last into the glass.

"What?"

"Prayed. Not like they do in churches, but *really* prayed? You done that?"

"I don't know," the girl said. "I talk to the Father-God."

He drank again. His small eyes lifted and caught hers, but immediately she bent over her soda.

He leaned close to her: "Whyn't you pray with us?"

"How?"

He watched her, waiting, but there was no further word from her: she sat silently staring into her glass.

He straightened up then, his voice louder and less intimate, and he began again, as if instructing a child:

"There's walls of fire that get built all around us so's we—" But suddenly he stopped and turned back to the bottle.

"Naw," he said. He looked long and broodingly at the bottle, and in a voice that startled all of the bar: "*Nawwwww.*"

Without looking at her, he waved his hand as if willing her away.

"Get out," he said.

She looked up startled: "What?"

"*GET OUT!*"

She got up and hurried out of the bar.

That was the first time. The second time she met them again in the bar. When she saw them coming she had ducked her head and started to go past them to the door (not daring to look up for fear he would catch her eyes), but he had stopped her. Wordlessly, holding her arm and pressing hard upon it, he pulled her to the same table where they sat in silence. Without a word, he snapped his fingers above his head as signal for the bottle; a beer was brought for the woman and they sat in silence. The girl leaned back in the shadows; the woman sat beneath the broad brim of her hat, now and then fingering her charm bracelets nervously with pudgy fingers. Her round face was like a doll's; vacuous. Like most whores of her class, there was one article of clothing the buying of which amounted to an obsession—in her case, umbrellas: she had dozens of them, of all sizes and colors (and one even, a red one, with a music box in the handle that played "April Showers" and that she had played incessantly for weeks after she had purchased it), was never seen without one, and even now one lay across the table in front of her: Jack and Jill and Humpty Dumpty and Old King Cole and Mary and Her Lamb and Little Bo Peep.

That night they waited until the bar was about to close. The bottle of scotch was empty, the woman was drunk, and the Prophet rose unsteadily from the table, drawing the girl up with him. They had not spoken in all of that time; now he stood looking round the bar, squinting with his little eyes as if myopic, or those others were too tiny for him to see. Then he turned to the woman and she heaved quickly but unsteadily to her feet as at a signal and stood beside the girl.

They stood side by side, a chorus—the bowed and stooped brooding girl, the huge, swaying Negro and the squat woman all in summer silks and pink petticoats and tiny, pointed red shoes on her doll's feet. The woman stood swaying for a moment, and then lifted her umbrella to her shoulder and opened it with a quick sound like a rush of wind; then the umbrella twirled at her shoulder as if in preparation for an afternoon stroll.

But it was night, dark midnight.

They left the bar and walked to their hotel. It was a cheap hotel and they ascended upon faded carpets in yellow light. Upon another faded carpet (birds here; worn by a million footsteps, dull-blue they soared in sudden tumult down the long hall: she felt she could almost hear the startled flappings of wings) and through a door in a long row of identical doors.

It was a large room. Here too was a carpet; and a small lamp upon the only table threw a ledge of light upon it. Against one wall was the bed, neatly made, the white sheets stretched tight like skin and an afghan coverlet folded down. The room was neat, immaculate, a home, and from the wall above the bed a framed Negro Jesus looked down benevolently. The woman was wearing a tight pink raincoat, and now she shed it like skin, picked up a knitting basket and sat beside the small lamp at the table. Immediately the girl was startled, for then a sudden sound broke the stillness; the sound became a rhythm; and when the girl looked furtively at her she saw her pumping gently and contentedly in the squeaking rocking-chair. She watched too as the woman bent over her basket and produced a long man's scarf. Her plump hands burrowed within the basket, brought out the needles and the end of the scarf, and with swift, certain motions took up the knitting. The lamp upon the table before her was small, throwing only that ledge of light onto the floor at her feet, and as the woman rocked gently with her knitting she moved from light to darkness, and back again.

The girl turned suddenly, frightened. Her head and shoulders lowered, her eyes took on that sullen, distrustful expression, and for a moment, in the dimly lighted room, she had the appearance of a miniature bull about to charge and pawing the ground. The Prophet stood in the middle of the room facing her. In the darkness his turban stood like a separate white head observing her. His chest was bare; it was completely covered with gray hair like fungus.

He came toward her, and the girl stumbled backward against the bed. "No," she said severely; then she lowered her head into her hands. She felt him sit down next to her on the bed, and then his hands were on her blouse, trying to unbutton it.

"I'm not gonna hurt you 'less I have to," he said.

"No": it came like a low scream this time— anguish and terror—and suddenly she was trembling uncontrollably.

"Not gonna hurt you now," his voice came again. He had unbuttoned the blouse and now she could feel him tugging at it, trying to draw it from around her shoulders; but her face was still lowered into her hands and he could not remove it. Almost gently, he tried to lower one of her arms, but she was still trembling, her hands pressed tight against her face. She heard him unzipper himself, and she knew without looking what he had done.

"Won't hurt you none," he was saying. "We'll just pray together now."

The squeaking of the chair stopped; she knew the woman had ceased her knitting and was looking up. "That's right, honey. He won't hurt. You just go on now." The squeaking resumed, and for a full minute there was only that sound, and the rest was silence.

Until suddenly: *Come on now*," and she felt the blow upon the side of her head and saw the quick flashes of light inside her head, and sprawled back upon the bed.

In a second he was on top of her. He was tearing at her clothing, her body. "Come on now, you know you want it," he was saying. "All you white chicks gotta have it sooner or later."

"That's true," the woman's voice came; then she resumed her rocking.

She felt she was smothering; for a moment his chest was pressed to her face, and she could taste the sweaty white hairs in her mouth. She could feel it then, hard and hot against her bare thighs, and then she opened her eyes and in desperate, final panic fought furiously. She reached up once, raking his face with her nails; and then again; but this time, missing, her hand clung to the turban, yanking it off, and for one insane moment with dreadful clarity it seemed she had ripped off the white top of his head, and as he bent his head down she recoiled, awaiting fearfully the spilling out of brains and blood over her.

But it never came; instead she lay staring up at his

completely bald head upon which were little bandages of reflected light. Looking into those small, beady eyes then, he seemed almost pitiful and ugly. She closed her own eyes, and that is when the blows came—slow; measured—one, two, three, four: there may have been a dozen before she lost consciousness.

When she awoke he was squatting naked and shivering in the farthest corner of the room. He sat upon his heels, the toes curled up and the gray bottoms of his feet below the brown ankles like half-rubbers. He sat as if unseeing, staring ahead at the patterned paper of the opposite wall, his naked buttocks strangely fat and child-like: as huge as he was, he looked pathetic huddling there, his lips blue in the pale light.

The woman still sat at the table, knitting; only now she wore her large picture hat against the light. Still rocking, she dipped squeaking into light—and out— buoy-like below the flat, large hat, the steel needles flashing and clicking like teeth at the edge of the lengthening scarf. "Would you like some tea, honey?" she asked, not looking up.

"No." She hugged her torn clothes to her, and, eyes narrowed to slits and face rigid with sudden-found hatred, glared across at the Negro.

The woman stopped rocking, looked up suddenly alarmed, and one fat, pink finger went to her lips as a warning:

"Be quiet now. He won't hurt you no more."

The girl sat as if dazed for a moment. All now was

55

more unreal than any of the dreams, and she watched in terror and amazement as the woman steadied her rocker, replaced her knitting in the basket and rose facing her. The round, freckled face smiled inanely below the large hat, her stubby arms held out to her from the pink whispering tulle blouse. Her eyes, above smooth perfect twin hillocks of cheeks, were transformed to ecstasy, beatific, as she started slowly toward her.

The girl sprang up from the bed. Head lowered, arms outstretched, she charged furiously to meet her, driving her arms into her bulging stomach. She felt the pillow of stomach deflate, sink like a burst balloon, heard the moaning rush of breath and saw the look of pained surprise. She saw the woman fall backward into the chair, the chair topple to the floor, the woman's legs rising up naked above her skirt as she plunged backward out of sight like a puppet yanked from its stage.

And she saw the Prophet, still squatting and staring ahead oblivious.

Then she rushed to the door and through it into the yellow light and the wild scurryings of birds.

That was when she took the apartment. The hundred dollar bill was used then: it paid three months' rent on the big, empty rooms. With what was left, she bought paints and brushes and the cheapest possible foods, including a fifty-pound sack of potatoes. The rest—the mattresses and furnishings and easel and cooking utensils—were given to her over a period of months.

No one visited her there; nor did she go out for the longest time except when necessary. All of the lights blazed in the rooms night and day; and when she was not painting, she would roam gloomily from bare room to bare room.

During the first week—before she was given a mattress—she slept in the large front room, curled tightly into one corner against the wall, as if allotting herself only the smallest place for sleep.

Only twice did she go out at night: once to roam the streets for an hour and pass, almost unseen, through one of the coffeehouses; and, invited then, once to that party on the desolate California coast.

4

He moved all of his furniture into her apartment. It was a happy day for him—a Saturday, bright and full of sunshine—and he instructed the movers carefully on where each piece of furniture was to be placed; he even paid one to hang his lace curtains and vermillion drapes before the large front window.

That day he wore an expensive, tasteful sport-shirt open at the neck, and a new gray lightweight gabardine suit, subdued but sporty, that even fit him, hiding as well as possible the knobby, long wrists and that he had paid eighty-five dollars for in honor of the occasion. The hat remained—the expensive gray Panama —but on this occasion, this Saturday afternoon, he wore it pushed slightly back; casual.

He tipped each of the moving men a dollar, and when they had left he and the girl stood silent for a moment in the midst of this strange new jungle. She had made no mention of getting rid of her old furniture—the mattresses, the battered crates disgorging old clothes and rags, the sagging couch with its tears and puffs of white stuffing—and he had not pressed the point; and so the two sets of furniture cohabited: the other, his, austere, gray, rigid—such as is found in homes where the shades are always drawn against afternoon sunlight. He had had the men lay the rugs first, and his furniture was carefully placed upon them, large and small pieces like an army at ease and curiously grouped round and inspecting a few ragged, surly strangers.

When they were alone he made an inspection of the rooms, she following silently behind. In the bedroom he took her into his arms. A rush of warmth came over him and he wanted to tell her something, but he did not know what to say; and so he patted her head and sent her off to prepare the dinner. She hesitated a moment, as if about to tell him something, then shrugged and stomped off into the kitchen.

He went into the front room and sat down on his own sofa. He had hung up his suitcoat in the front room closet: it was empty. She had evidently never thought of storing away her things there, for filigrees of cobwebs hung from each corner; dust-heavy newspapers lined the shelf. The floor was covered with dust, and as he stepped back he saw the footprints his new tan loafers with the foam rubber soles had made there. He looked down once at the prints in the sheet of dust, then backed out of the closet, closing the door upon them. Now he placed his hat carefully upon the coffee table, turned up his shirt sleeves, and sat waiting.

He sighed with contentment, looking round the

room, dreaming. He saw the girl upon his arm at a company party—in a new dress and with earrings; white gloves. They moved casually among the executives, nodding to the slim, balding men and their pretty wives; and later entertaining Mr. Riggs, the Personnel Manager, and his wife, who drank, serving martinis, offering cigars from a scented humidor. . . . He got up smiling and went into the kitchen.

She had not even started to prepare dinner. She sat in the middle of the kitchen upon a high stool, her chin cupped in the bowl of her hand, hunched over and watching a cockroach scurrying along the baseboard: she could not cook. Her legs drawn up, the big red smock covered her sneakered feet. She looked out gloomily now, and he went to her and placed his arms around her shoulders. He felt love, compassion, tenderness; and he nestled her dark head against his chest. Her head burrowed there, as if seeking something; his knobby fingers moved over her, stroking it.

He made the dinner that night, and when they had finished eating and done the dishes he sent her into the bedroom. He went into the bathroom then, spending twenty minutes before the cracked mirror preparing himself. The bathroom was dirty: a naked bulb hung there too; and beside the gurgling toilet a pile of wet rags. He studied himself in the mirror a moment. He was wearing new pajamas too, rayon ones with tasteful colored flowers upon them —and between trembling and delight he managed to find the string dangling raveled from the ceiling, turn off the light and go into the hall.

He hurried down the uncarpeted corridor in his bare feet. When he reached the room, he saw her sitting up in the center of the large bed between lavender sheets. He could tell she was naked beneath the sheet, and she sat as she had upon the stool in the kitchen—her knees drawn up and her head lowered onto them—utterly lost and improbable there.

He hurried across the floor to her.

He could not touch her. Night after night she just lay there, and he knew she was thinking of something else, or nothing at all. It was as if he were hardly there at all for her, and for long periods at night he watched her roaming from blazing room to blazing room. She would not sleep at night, but leave the bed as soon as it was over, put on her sneakers and the red smock and wander off through the rooms or sit silently folded into a ball on her couch in the front room. For her there was no night or day, no destination, no ordering of hours; when she did sleep, it could be at any time, or at any place in any of the rooms. And always, even sleeping, dressed in the sneakers and the red smock.

He would arrive bleary-eyed at his desk in the morning, move sluggishly through the day. After a few weeks of this he saw the other clerks watching him suspiciously; remarks were dropped intended for his ears; and when finally Mr. Riggs passed his desk slowly, seemingly on some other business but, he knew, watching him critically, then with a shock he understood: *they thought he had begun to be a drunkard.*

And what was strange: he *was* drinking at night now; more often than he ever had, but not really drunk often. He would sit across from her in the big front room at night drinking beer from quart bottles. He seldom drank anything stronger than beer; he had reasoned years before that he could not become a drunkard if he followed this rule. Now and then she would go to her easel and paint, and he would watch her. The paintings were always the same—those small, furry, frightened animals with large haunted eyes hiding in dense jungles; only now the jungles had begun to take on the features of cities: slowly, in painting after painting, buildings had become visible, gray monoliths like leafless stone plants thrusting upwards through the dense vines and foliage; here and there a light, pale as a faded moon; a telephone pole; white stone houses like tombstones. After a while he realized he could no longer distinguish jungle from city. But the animals were still there—crouched in doorways and among vines.

But he did not often get really drunk. He would drink perhaps two quarts of beer and then sleep. He would not sleep long, and when he awoke she would be in another room, and he would follow her then, sipping beer again until again he would doze. On several nights he followed her in that way, taking only his bottle of beer and glass with him each time. During that period, night after night, they slept and lived in all of the rooms—he following—and although they made love often, and whenever he wished, it was more often upon one of the floors or mattresses or the couches than in the bed. The large bed, with its unaccustomed pillows and lavender sheets, frightened her; she seemed wary of it, approached it cautiously, as if it were some dangerous sleeping animal.

It was at that time, a month after he had moved into the apartment, that he had bought the robe. Afterwards, he had justified the purchase by telling himself it was a perfectly reasonable thing to do; for if he was to sit night after night in those rooms, what better purchase than a lounging robe?

A Saturday again; bright and warm; and he had gone to the park across from St. Francis at first to shake his hangover. Being Friday, he had drunk more than usual the night before—nearly three quarts —and when he had awakened upon the couch five hours later he had still been a little drunk and not able to go back to sleep in the bed. For the first time he had awakened with that feeling that nearly every heavy drinker knows on the following day of leisure —a fear really: what was he to do with the day, how dispose of it? It stretched before him, an unnerving waste. It was frightening, inexplicable: never before

63

had he thought of *disposing* of hours; by principle, logic and what he thought of as temperament he had always accepted hours of leisure quite naturally to be used, to serve him; and now they were this waste, the day a sun-pounded wilderness that at any cost must be filled, occupied, populated. He had shaved and dressed, trembling from both the lingering effects of drunkenness and this new frenzy, glanced at the girl once as she lay curled up and sleeping upon a mattress, and then gone trembling and slightly nauseous onto the sun-heavy street.

He had sat in the park until early afternoon, but under the bright sun on that breezeless day the hangover had persisted, the anxiety increased. Again he wore the new gabardine suit, now slightly rumpled, his trousers pulled up carefully above shiny loafers and bright argyle socks. His normally healthy, tanned face was now almost red from fever and sun, and his coarse hair dry and straw-colored: his skin was very sensitive to sun, and each summer, he knew, would bring him more than his share of sunburn.

Finally he had gotten up and strolled along the shaded side of Grant Avenue, past the very bars and coffeehouses the girl had told him about in her story. He had stopped briefly before one window—a men's furnishings store—and been impressed: arranged in the window with feminine delicacy were all of the articles of clothing he had never before dared purchase: flagrantly colored waistcoats, hand-carved belts, Tyrolean hats, bright fluffed ascots; and, in the center, a large oriental lounging robe with full wide sleeves like wings and winding bright dragons upon them: it lay spread out among the other things as if it had descended suddenly to casual repose. He thought it beautiful: he imagined himself lounging gracefully upon the couch in it, a cigarette holder held delicately extended and discoursing to his admiring company. It was such a robe as George Sanders, of the movies, might wear. For a moment he became George Sanders, and when he looked up it was in embarrassment, for one of the two clerks, or owners, of the small shop was looking through the window at him smiling—a delicate, tall young man with streaks of bleached blond like rivers through his sandy hair, and a slim, girlish body in tightly fitted slacks. Another man, older, stooped and graying but bearing a curious resemblance to the younger one, was directly behind him lounging upon the counter and looking out at Farley with a tired, collapsed face just short of boredom. The younger man signalled for Farley to come into the shop, but he pretended not to see, and turning awkwardly hurried down the street.

It was afternoon then, the sun was hot, the hangover and that nervous expectancy persisted, and as he approached one dark, cool-looking bar he turned suddenly in, sat at the bar and ordered a beer: it was the first time in his life he had ever drunk during the day to rid himself of a hangover. He sat at the bar sipping his beer. It was one of the bars the girl had told him about: all around him were the bearded men and the sharp-featured, barracudic women. He drank another beer, and in half an hour, over his third beer, he was almost peaceful: he smiled benignly at several of the people and settled comfortably on his stool. It did not bother him or really occur to him that none had smiled back.

It was cool in the bar; dark; and within an hour the hangover was gone, and with it the feeling of frenzy. In a little while he was happy sitting there, and he sat tapping his fingers upon the bar and sipping his beers casually. A feeling of well-being came over him with the beers; he had not spoken to anyone, but he felt as if he had found a sort of home there. He did not understand it, but then he did not question it either. Now and then one of the intense young men would come from their tables to the bar to buy beers, and twice he had leaned over and asked if he might treat: the muttered, hasty thanks of each had been waved aside magnanimously with a sweep of his hand.

He knew he was getting drunk, but that did not matter. Lighting a cigarette, he sat waving and tapping it between his extended fingers, as if he were smoking it from a long holder.

For as long as he could remember, Farley had had what to him was a slightly shameful vice: the movies. For periods, he would go to as many as ten movies a week. Secretly; stealthily. He would have been ashamed to be discovered in this passion, and yet it was his strongest passion, and a comfort. The darkness had hidden him, soothed him; and in the figures upon the screen he lived a secret but passionate existence. He would emerge from each theatre, for hours at a time the tall, virile John Wayne; the nasal, terrifying Peter Lorre; the sophisticated and graceful Fred Astaire. Now, in that cool, dark bar, in drunkenness, he became George Sanders: when he spoke to the bartender, ordering another beer, it was in the cynical, world-weary and sexual tones of the actor; his eyebrows lifted and fell tiredly in sophisticated contemplation of the world. The words were not there, the thoughts, but in drunkenness and dream there was the *feeling* of ironic comment upon that world: once he even waved his hand with the imagined long holder the length of the bar with weary, amused tolerance.

He *became* George Sanders: he staggered once to the men's room, bumping into a girl: "Pardon me, my dear," he said, bowing, and returning from there he had moved through the now-crowded late-afternoon bar waving his free hand (in the other was the imagined cigarette holder), brushing aside imagined obstacles of human flesh as he made his way back to the stool.

When he was properly drunk he made his decision, slid from the stool and staggered onto the street. It had been dusk then, the sky overcast with heavy fists of dark rainclouds: the street, the sky were gray, washed dull and lifeless by an impending storm. Now and then the dying sun would flicker behind clouds

67

like a brief, spent bulb—and disappear: the shadow of a cloud would pass over the street like a swift dark hand caressing it.

He hurried into the small men's furnishings store, standing breathless from running but suddenly still and embarrassed before the younger of the two clerks. Silent, weaving slightly from side to side in drunkenness, he had pointed to the robe in the darkening window.

The young clerk smiled; he turned; and, with movements that in Farley's drunkenness reminded him of a footed snake, patted upon leather soles almost upon his toes to a rack; then came back—but slowly, the upper portion of his body swaying with an odd grace. He stood before Farley, the robe draped over his delicate outstretched arms.

"It's lovely, my dear," the young man said. "Quite chic. Just the thing for intimate parties."

Farley looked up suddenly into the young man's face: it was pasty white, the eyes dark and tired. The corners of his delicate mouth turned down in approximation of a smile: it was like a white, cracked mask in the dim light of the darkening shop: above it, the short hair was combed down over his forehead in bangs, three precise rivers of bleached blond falling from his forehead as from a waterfall; not one hair out of place, so that it appeared to be a wig above the mask of face. When he looked again, the young man was holding out the robe to him, his thin fingers upon each shoulder like bird's claws.

"No no," Farley said in confusion, meaning he did not want to try it on there. "Fine. Wrap it."

With something like a sigh, or an expression of distaste, the young man turned and patted to the counter. He produced a box and tissue paper, laying the robe carefully inside. He folded the edges of the paper slowly over the robe, as one would fold a sheet over a dead body, and closed the lid.

"That too," Farley said, pointing. He indicated a black cigarette holder in the case below the counter: an imitation diamond was the only ornament. The clerk produced a small box, and more tissue paper, and the careful entombment was repeated with the cigarette holder. Then the smiling white mask of a face looked up at him; it started to speak, but Farley had flung the money onto the counter, taken up the packages and was on his way to the door.

"Come again, dear," he heard the voice call as he lunged through the door onto the street.

When he got back to the bar he got very drunk. He unwrapped the cigarette holder and sat smoking on his stool. He was happy; he felt secure in the dark bar; cut off from the world.

His only dissatisfaction was that there was no one to show the robe to: he did not know anyone in the bar. He gave himself up to imagination, became George Sanders again, and drank, holding the large box upon his knees. A boy came to the bar and sat next to him staring dismally down into his hands; and he bought him a beer. He sat swaying upon his stool through two beers, watching the boy with his George Sanders look, before he asked the boy's name. The boy mumbled something that Farley could not distinguish as any name; but he nodded, as if the boy's incoherent response had revealed some profound truth to him; paused long enough to puff reflectively upon his cigarette holder, and was about to speak again when the boy turned without a word and disappeared into one of the dark corners of the bar.

He got very drunk. At the end of the evening he was so drunk he could hardly sit up; but he was happy.

Around midnight he stumbled through the streets back to the apartment, the box smashed down and clutched under his arm. When he knocked at the door, Lenore did not answer; it was locked. He waited, silent and listening in the dim hallway. He could see the light beneath the door, and he waited a long time, and now and then he could hear her moving from room to room, but she did not answer. He knocked again, louder, but still she did not answer, although he could still hear her moving among the rooms.

It did not bother him. Standing swaying against the wall, he knew that if he knocked loud enough, and often enough, she would hear him in time and let him in; but instead he preferred to settle down in the hall for the night. He liked the idea: it was his night, his dream; why should he share it with her? Humming to himself, his back pressed to the wall to keep from falling, and now and then sliding almost to his knees, or swaying perilously forward upon his toes, he managed to rip open the box; and throwing the pieces of cardboard and crumpled fists of tissue paper like huge snowflakes around him, he finally freed the robe and held it in front of him with an ecstatic rush of breath: it was beautiful. A slithering green dragon wound down each sleeve to the cuffs, breathing red flames.

Nearly falling twice—slowly, tenderly—he managed at last to draw the robe around him. He reached into his right-hand back trouser pocket and withdrew the newly laundered handkerchief he always carried, inserting it rakishly into the breast pocket of the robe.

And only then did he sink to the floor. He placed another cigarette in his holder, lighted it and sat smoking. His eyes closed for a minute, and when he shook himself suddenly awake he was stretched out nearly full length upon the floor. The hall was deserted, and nearly soundless except for the girl moving in her voyagings from room to room.

After that he went to bars several times a week; and always he would return drunk; and always he would be a little late, and hung over, the next day at work.

He would sit with her at night in his new robe drinking the beer. It had not been the same the next morning, when he had looked at the robe sober: it had seemed cheap to him then, gaudy. The robe had become rumpled and a little dirty from his night in the hall; and, worse, the next morning, hung over and sick, when the girl opened the door and found him there in the hall, he had stumbled almost blindly and in shame hurriedly through the door, catching one of the wide, deep pockets on the doorknob and ripping it nearly off.

But, as disreputable and removed from dream as the robe had become, it still served the purpose for which it was bought. One evening the girl remarked, "She had a robe like that."

"Who?"

"The big woman. Thorn."

"Oh."

He was upon her torn couch, and she sat cross-legged upon the floor before him.

"Hers had dragons too," the girl said. "And the sleeves were like wings; big bird's wings that flapped all over the house. It was silk, though, and it swished whenever she walked. I could hear her coming from rooms away, like whispers, voices."

She reached down and began picking dead skin from the heels of her feet, flicking the pieces out invisibly around her, absorbed. He watched with squeamish attention, only turning away at the moment the dead skin became separated from the healthy flesh. He watched fascinated a last time, and then looked away from it, shuddering.

After the second month, along with the piles of furniture, there were quart beer bottles in every room, nearly always upon the floor—over a hundred of them. Most of the bottles stood against one wall in the front room—a formidable collection—but others were scattered or stood all over the room, where they were knocked from place to place during Farley's and the girl's incessant wanderings.

Which was strange; for before he had always been a meticulous, a neurotic housekeeper: an item of furniture out of place, an overlooked area of dirt would cause in him something like panic; and if, for some reason, he could not remedy the imperfection immediately the panic would follow him through the day, his mind would return constantly to it and he would be plagued by a nervous anxiety that on one occasion even destroyed his appetite, causing him to leave untouched a ninety-cent lunch. At the end of the day he rushed back to the apartment with the same morbid preoccupation a husband might feel in rushing back to a suspected unfaithful wife.

So that for Farley to grow a beard was the last thing anyone would have expected of him.

The Prophet had started him: he had seen the Prophet and the little whore in one of the bars and the Prophet had begun a beard of his own. The beard was not fully grown, but already it was hideous: it grew in long, uneven, wire-like black strands, and the moustache drooped down over his mouth like Genghis Khan's. The hair was sparse, widely spaced, so that it looked more like a fan of moss falling nearly square at the end to below his chin.

The Prophet and the whore sat at their usual table with some others; and Farley hovered drunk in the distance around them. He got drunker than usual that

73

night, and when the Prophet and the whore left, he left too.

He followed them. The Prophet staggered and stumbled all the way, and now and then the little whore would support him. As Farley watched from a distance, it was a strange scene: the big man would lurch and nearly lose his balance in drunkenness, and the plump little whore would rush to him and, too short to support him by the arms, push him up by the waist. The Prophet's arms would flail out above his head insanely, as if driving away a horde of insects in that night, and then he would shove off the little whore and she would stagger a few feet and follow silent and cowed; until again he staggered, and she would rush in and steady him; and again he would drive her off: upon that dark nightstreet it was like some shadow joined and separating endlessly.

Farley followed them to their hotel. It was the hotel the girl had told him about, and when they were gone he stood for a long time in the street looking up at the dark, closed windows.

That night he went back to the apartment and made passionate love to the girl. He prided himself that she thought it was sudden love for her that prompted it; but she did not suspect that for a minute.

A month after that, Farley lay stretched naked upon his stomach on the floor of the front room. He lay full length upon the mattress, a quart bottle of beer on the floor at his head. The girl sat crosslegged beside him, now and then leaning forward and applying with curious, detached fury suntan lotion to his hairless, naked body.

The beard had started to grow; it had just begun to take shape—light brown with a tint of auburn.

"I saw the Prophet," he said at last. He had not told her before.

She did not answer. Bent over him, her face pressed close to his back, she looked as if she were examining him for insects.

"He was with the blonde whore. . . . Will you do that for me?"

"No."

He turned onto his back, looking up at her. "You used to," he said.

"You always ask me now. Before you never used to ask me."

"I haven't asked you for a while."

"I don't like to talk about it," she said. "I'm busy with other things."

He got up onto his elbows. "I haven't asked you for a week. Now have I? Tell the truth. Hasn't it been a week? A whole week?"

"You said last time you wouldn't ask me any more."

"Well, it's been a week," he persisted. "You've got to admit that."

He lay back again as she poured some more of the suntan lotion from the bottle and started rubbing it into his chest, bent over and working vigorously.

"Oh," he sighed, giving a little shudder of pleasure.

"That's nice. Yes. There . . . uhhh . . . oh yes. That's good. Oh!" He grabbed her hand suddenly to make her stop, and she sat still, bent over him, frozen there as he lay back tensely. He gave a little, sudden shudder, and then relaxed, sighing. After a moment, he began speaking again—his voice low, his eyes closed:

"I burn easily," he said dreamily. "Every year I get burned if I'm not careful. It runs in the family. We're all very sensitive to sun. . . . Do you love me?" he asked suddenly; but she did not answer and he did not really expect her to. "What do you think he does with the blonde whore?" he asked after a while.

"I don't know," the girl said.

He opened one eye, looking up at her suspiciously. "Didn't he ever tell you?"

"No."

"Nothing?"

"No." . . . "I'm going now," she finally said. "I have a lot to do."

He sighed, and the eye dropped closed and he lay silent for a while.

She shrugged, capped the bottle of lotion and got up. With sudden darkness, she plunged down broodingly onto her couch. She sat with her eyes narrowed nearly to slits, biting fiercely upon her thumbnail.

He opened his eyes and sat quickly up. "Don't do that, Lenore. Don't go into one of your moods. I can see it coming."

She jerked her hand from her mouth, seemed for a moment to be fighting something within herself, and then relaxed a little.

"All right," she said.

"That's better," he said. "You can be nice when you want to."

He put on his robe, got up and stood before his wall mirror, inspecting himself.

"The beard's coming along nicely," he said.

"Yes."

He straightened his shoulders and turned swiftly from the mirror, at the same time swinging out the robe as if it were a cape. He sat down next to her and put his arm around her. They were both silent for a long time, and when she felt him starting to breathe heavily she shut her eyes tight, as if against a bright light. When he spoke, she had achieved complete darkness, cut off:

"Lenore—"

"Yes?"

"Please?"

"No," she said sharply.

He sighed then, got up and stood before the mirror again admiring his image. He threw back his head to see the beard more clearly, then lowered it. It was a long time before he spoke again, but when he did it was with a sort of condescension.

"All right," he said. "It was beginning to bore me anyway."

He began to walk off haughtily, but no sooner was

77

he in the hallway than he heard, distinctly, his own voice with frightening exactness, like an echo, uttering that last sentence again:

"*All right. It was beginning to bore me anyway.*"

He back-stepped quickly and looked into the room. But there was only the girl, alone.

He went to the bars more and more: it was a place to be.

He began to wear shoestring ties, and within another month his beard had asserted itself to become a scraggly and indifferent mass of red-tinted hairs that in spite of all his care looked strange and ridiculous: like the false beard of a stage Russian. He had become known to a group of penniless poets, bought drinks for them; and it was at their table that he was most often seen. He even wrote some poetry himself, but he did not show it to any of them: he was secretly ashamed because it rhymed. One night, apropos of nothing, and even before he had known what he was about to say, he had broken his usual silence and declared to the table of poets, all of whom always talked of their discontented generation, "We are all the great herd of the new migration."

Perhaps he had heard it somewhere, or read it; he could never remember. But under the circumstances it was a stroke of brilliance: it correctly characterized, and therefore legitimatized, a state of chaos. At any rate, he thought it brilliant if no one else did, and that night he had gone home happy, and almost trembling.

But Farley could not assimilate guilt as others do, and so there were shadows, ghosts. He had not really the ability to rationalize guilt in terms of personal necessity; he could only fear it. He was on his way to becoming a sort of drunkard of the spirit. He would fight his lust, thinking it shameful; and then, in a fearful rush of weakness, indulge in it. Like the drunkard, repentance would follow, in which he would try to make it up to her, inundate her with kindnesses and a kind of love and tenderness which was never expiatory since it was himself he sought forgiveness from; followed by a period of abstinence—and then the rush to lust, a joy actually, with just the shadow of anticipated guilt.

At his job they were aghast. In less than six months the change was startling. He was aware of their puzzlement, the comments and their feelings of uneasiness in his presence. At first there had been the drinking, the frequent and increasing hangovers, the even relieved feeling among them then that that hard edge of stiffness and unreality had worn off of him and that at last he approximated something human; and then the beard, and even this tolerated to an extent as a youthful indulgence: his job was at a desk, in an inner office with other clerks, and since he did not ever come into contact with the public, the beard was just mildly frowned upon; and then the clothes: he still wore the Ivy League suits (he could not have afforded a new wardrobe in any case), but now they were often unpressed, even baggy, not wholly from neglect they were certain, but, if they had been able to admit it, believe in and formulate the idea (which they could not wholly, since it implied a repudiation among the ranks and an actual indictment of themselves), contempt. Now and then he wore a shoestring tie. Gone were the umbrella and the hat, and his now long and unbarbered hair curled down over his collar in quarter moons.

But it was not so much his clothes that bothered them as his general attitude and bearing: that stiff, shell-like quality that had before characterized him had disappeared. Now he walked nearly slouched; withdrawn and indifferent and moody. Seldom now was heard from him a "Good morning," the eternal affirmation among them, the exacted ritual lie that was their comfort: more often than not, he would even ignore their morning greetings and go silently to his desk among disapproving stares. But more, and finally, there was the feeling now of contempt.

Among the clerks in his office there was a little hunchback. Except in matters pertaining to the office—and then always curtly, sullenly—the little man almost never spoke to anyone there: he sat upon a thick cushion at his desk, working with a silent absorption that did not conceal the bitterness and hatred he felt for the job and all those around him. Each morning he assembled his materials for the day's work—sharpened pencils, pens, ruler, stapler, scratch pad, erasers, a jar of rubber bands and paper clips: an army ready for the assault—and when he began punc-

tually at nine, there was seldom a pause or an inter-
ruption. No one spoke to him when it was not necessary; nor was he ever known to address a civil word to
any of them; but now and then he would look up from
his work, his small, deformed body high upon the
cushioned chair, his legs dangling in children's shoes
and trousers like a child's, and his head before the
large hump peering out darkly. Farley had always
shuddered when those cold eyes had caught his. To
him, the man was like a huge, ugly spider perched
there—malevolent and ubiquitous.

He lived in a furnished room, Farley knew, and yet
strangely the little man carried upon a key chain on
a heavy brass ring perhaps a hundred keys. What most
of the keys were for, Farley did not know, but two of
them were for his desk, and each night he would clear
the desk until it was bare even of blotter and calendar,
and even the tall cushion he sat upon would be stuffed
into one of the drawers and locked up with the rest
of his possessions for the night; and then he would
slip the keys onto a metal clasp on his belt and hobble
silent and bent over out of the office.

One night he did not leave the office immediately;
instead, he turned and made his way slowly between
the desks toward Farley. His little legs could barely
support him, and he walked stooped over and twisting
laboriously from side to side; and as Farley watched, it
was more than ever the spider—some huge, crippled
spider dragging itself across the floor toward him.
Farley watched each groaning, twisting step until he

was before his desk. A book was lying upon the desk—poetry—and the little man reached over and carefully lifted the book, inspecting it as if it were alive, and offensive to him. When he had satisfied his curiosity, he held the book at arm's length above the desk by two fingers disdainfully, and then dropped it.

He had to look up to catch Farley's eyes then. "Poetry," he sneered in a mincing voice. He turned and hobbled slowly to the door, Farley watching him in silence; and when he reached the door, he turned and spoke again, his voice loud and clear and insinuating across the long rows of desks:

"Lordy me, *poetry!*"—and was gone.

Once he came to the office drunk. They looked at him, and he knew they knew. He dropped papers from his desk in profusion; fumbled for objects that were in front of him; and, although he tried not to, staggered perceptibly the dozen or so times he left his desk to go to the men's room.

The hunchback seemed to scurry then even more: he was everywhere around Farley—ostensibly on business around the office, but circling Farley again and again as if spinning a web around him. Finally he became so sick with the circlings of the energetic little man that he made another trip to the men's room and sat inside the locked cubicle for a full fifteen minutes: the day seemed endless—full of taut nerves and nausea and frenzy.

He had drunk that night until it was time to go to

work, and was forced to sober up awake. In drunken exuberance, he had told one of the secretaries—an imperious young woman with whom he had until then not been the least bit friendly—with a sly and conspiratorial wink, that he had been up all night making love to his mistress. He had liked the sound of that word, and had thought lovingly of it and the impression he was certain it had made; but in the afternoon, when he remembered it, and remembered too the cold, contemptuous response it had actually elicited—then he had been sick with shame.

At the end of the day he swore it would not happen again; but by night his nerves and the anxiety and shame for what he had done and said was so strong that he went out again to the bars.

The next day he did not arrive at work until noon; but that time he did not offer any excuse; he sat at his desk working as best he could. But there was something cold about him then—distant and impervious and with a dark, angry edge. It was not until later, until he was fired, that they discovered what he had carved that day with his steel letter opener into the bottom of one of the drawers. It was crude, but positive:

MOTHERFUCKERS

It seemed to Farley that the day he was fired the little hunchback had known it before anyone; at least that was the thought that haunted him.

83

He was not really fired; he was "laid off" indefinitely as part of a "necessary reduction in force."

It was Mr. Riggs, Personnel Manager, who called him in. He sat large and flushed and asthmatic behind his desk—all big, angular bones thrusting for release below his cracked, parchment-like skin. Two white-capped waves of thinning hair rose uneasily to pompadours from the razor-straight valley of a part; and a thin, dapper moustache upon which was always seen a bead of sweat, like a secreted but ornamental pearl.

It was all very polite: "they" were sorry to see him go. Mr. Riggs sat with his large, flushed and sweating hands extended palms down and pressed flat against his desk blotter, as if preparing for the effort of pushing himself onto his feet; and when he finally did rise that is exactly what he did, leaving the imprint of palms and shattered, skeletal fingers upon the blotter. He also stared, it seemed, fascinated, into Farley's scraggly beard as he spoke. The man hardly once looked Farley in the eyes, all of the time speaking into the beard, so that the younger man had the uncomfortable feeling it was not he Mr. Riggs was addressing, but the beard. The man drank too much, and had high blood pressure too, so that the baked, coarse skin of his face and neck and hands seemed to glow, as if a fire burned beneath the skin.

All very polite and civilized and devious: Farley had become the symbol of unrest, the maverick, the now-revealed dark aberrant beast—diseased and corrupted and contaminating—and therefore voted to excommunication: in the most literal sense, exorcised. He sat distracted and half dreaming before the older man, observing now and then curiously a muscle—a nervous tic—that fluttered above the man's right cheek, as if some worm-like creature were imprisoned there beneath the skin and struggling for release; while Mr. Riggs stared as if hypnotized into Farley's beard. Farley felt sorry for the man then; for a moment he felt like reaching over and patting him consolingly upon the shoulder, but restrained himself. He kept nodding his head and agreeing and repeating again and again, idiotically, "I understand": it was like a song they were singing together—Farley supplying the chorus, and Mr. Riggs the verse:

"I'm sure you understand, Farley."

"I understand."

"You understand our position, Farley."

"I understand."

Farley suppressed an insane impulse to *sing* this last to the man: tremulous, like Jeanette MacDonald to Nelson Eddy during a love duet.

He went to his desk and packed his few possessions. The hunchback sat upon his cushioned seat, his doll's legs dangling and his square-toed child's shoes polished and waxed to mirror brightness. The hunchback sat actually above all of the others in the long row of desks: tiny legs and arms and disproportionately large trunk and head—a giant insect perched there above the bent heads; and Farley had the sudden image of the intense little creature scrambling suddenly upward, arms and legs flailing like a spider's, upon an invisible thread to the ceiling, and dangling there above their heads.

5

That was when Farley gave the party; a party to which no one came on the roof of the old building. A dream: a deserted and ravaged miniature golf course stood there.

But first he got a job; it lasted a week. He was assigned a desk, and he sat at it glowering at the other clerks. He had shaved the beard, but in that cracked mirror had emerged another face—darker and older and almost ravaged—as if it had grown secret and incontinent there all of those months.

He came each morning hunched over to the small office. A middle-aged woman dragged sluggishly with what would appear the weight of a hundred heavy years past his desk time after time, looking angrily at him. He knew she resented him; there was something in him now that was dense and unfriendly. The woman was mad: her graying hair was piled high upon her head like a hornet's nest from which a dozen wisps of hairs looked out like the lashes of secreted eyes; and her wild eyes would look up from her work now and then and search every inch of that dark, musty office with insane intensity. Once she had a fit there, and the two other clerks, pale and balding elderly men, carried her between them into the lavatory. They were all three sexless; there was no such thing as modesty involved: one took her head and the other her legs and, as frail as she was, the two old men struggled under her weight, the one holding a leg on each hip as if employing giant scissors; and as they moved out of the office, Farley could see the woman's skinny, pale thighs and her gray underclothes; and when they were gone he had sat breathing heavily and looking down sightlessly at his desk.

He sat glowering at that desk until he was fired. He could not help it; it was as if a fear, a paralysis had taken control of him and he could only wait as if turned to stone and imbedded there. The office was hidden—imbedded too—in the viscera of an old building: the windows looked out grayly onto a fire escape and a brick wall; no sun; and so all day bulbs burned dangling below tin shades, and upon each window heavy with a hundred blasted moons of dust each bulb was reflected like dead, glacial suns: his own reflection, heavy-shouldered and rooted, came back to him out of that lightless world; and with it the others—sluggish, deformed, elongated. When he was finally fired, he ran with voiceless, passionate joy for five blocks in the bright, sunlit street.

He sold the Volkswagen. It occurred to him that since they had first come to live together they had not once used it: they had never gone anywhere far enough away to need to use it. There had been nearly two hundred dollars in the bank, but that was soon gone; and when it was, and money was needed, the little car was the logical choice.

He had been fond of it. It had been one of his first important acquisitions; the first had been the apartment, and even that he had not been as proud of as he was the car. For the former, he had had a sort of passionless love—a pride, really, dry and secure, as a parent might feel for an honorable and moral son; but for the latter there was a feeling that was more intense, almost carnal. He had bought it second hand—a sporty little car, unlike any the men he admired and worked with, with the exception of those high and powerful enough to be allowed indulgences, possessed. It had indeed at the time seemed an indulgence; but one he could not resist. It was like that other vice, the movies; and one he also kept a secret from his associates and superiors, going to and from work each day by bus so that none of them even knew he owned it.

But now he sold it. The girl agreed by silence; she did not care one way or the other, and went on about her silent, gloomy and objectiveless life the same as ever. She did not even care that he had lost the job, any more than she had cared when he had lost the first one. For this he was grateful; a weight had been lifted from him, and since she ate practically nothing, and did not seek any amusement that cost money, she was not a burdensome responsibility. He was almost happy then; he was free.

The used-car dealer sat before his desk in the small office. It was really a shack, dingy and gray, with a pot-bellied stove and a rolltop desk and a stained coffee cup. He was a huge fat man: his buttocks hung over the stool he sat on, nearly obscuring it. He had dainty pink hands like a child's, and a hairless face vacuous and round as a moon: only his heavy, dark eyebrows, like fur pieces in the shapes of half moons, gave that face any of the character of a human being; for the eyes, hidden beneath deep furrows of flesh, were seldom seen. At first, Farley thought that face eyeless, and then the furrows parted, and the little eyes looked out a moment—blue and strangely lifeless—as if possessing an intelligence apart from the huge body; and then receded back into their graves of flesh. It was as if a separate, slow, passionless animal existed within him.

The huge man groaned up from his stool: every board in that shack floor creaked under him. He did not speak; perhaps he couldn't; but moving his mountainous body with slow, dragging steps and little wheezing sounds, he moved forward. He seemed to be twisting there upon the floor, making his progress across the shack by a pendulous, swinging movement, as if his huge legs and tiny feet were useless to him and he could only move by means of a sort of centrifugal propulsion.

At last they stood in the lot before the little car; the man moved slowly around it as Farley waited. Because of the fat, the man's massive arms were nearly extended, the pink child's hands like knobs: he looked for a moment like an idiot massive bird about to flap its wings and fly off; and as he moved, now and then one of the arms would swing slowly out, and, one tiny finger extended, probe the car; as if it were alive.

When he had circled the car, the man stood again beside Farley. For a moment, he looked almost sad; he stood dwarfing the little car; and Farley, in sudden panic, had the impression that he would reach over and pick it up like a toy and go off with it without a word. But he didn't; instead, that face started to work again, as if a machine had been started within it; the furrows drew up like shades, and those small, blue eyes were visible again, looking out at Farley curiously dead. One hand lifted and showed four fingers; and Farley agreed silently with a nod of his head.

It was as if a signal had been given—either the lifting of the huge man's four fingers (which might well have been some aberrant benediction) or Farley's nod of agreement—for across the gravelled lot, stooped over and dragging his feet, came a young Spaniard. His oily hair shone as unruffled and tight as black silk stretched across his skull; and a cross as large as a man's hand dangled before him upon a long chain from his neck. The cross glinted in the sun, the dark man stooped above it as if bowed by its inordinate weight. He did not even straighten up when he took the keys from Farley, or when he stepped into the car to drive it off. The car moved round the shack, and out of sight, the dark Spaniard pressed over the wheel like a dead man as he drove.

The fat man turned and moved toward the shack again, and Farley followed.

So that now Farley gave the party: it had been a dream of his.

On the roof of the old building in which they lived.

During the building's more prosperous days, the owner—an impractical, a singular, a whimsical man; a poet of sorts—had installed a miniature golf course there. Exposed to the elements and the ravages of former tenants and time, there was not much left of it; and what there was was in a hopeless state of devastation and disrepair: rotting and splintered and faded by rain, it was a sort of bleak and petrified roof garden three stories above the city, where all around a dozen hills rose, stuck with white hidden houses.

So that now the party was given: he made outlandish preparations. He bought food and whiskey and wine and little paper hats; he brought all of the chairs and cushions onto the roof, and on two tables he arranged the food and drink—enough for fifty people. He was happy; preparing for the party kept him busy; and as he worked at it, he drank. The afternoon before the party he bought pink paper plates and napkins and cups and forks and spoons; he set a place before each chair and cushion, and the others scattered over all of the roof; and set out the bowls of food and the drink six hours before the party was to begin.

The girl watched curiously: she was certain he was mad; and when he brought out all of his old copies of *Time* and *Newsweek* and placed them conveniently about the scene of the party, she was convinced. Alone there, as she watched from the stairway, he went from place to place, muttering as if in conversation with his anticipated guests.

But no one came. He had sent an invitation to one of the bars to be posted there, but it had never appeared. The invitation had read:

GIANT PARTY!
Refreshments! Entertainment!
On the Roof Garden
of
F. Grimm

and the date and address; but no one came.

At ten o'clock he sat out on the roof alone. He wore the Chinese robe and he smoked cigarettes through his long holder. He sat on one of his own chairs—a high, stiff-backed chair with wooden arms in the shapes of lion's claws. A mist moved over the city and the Bay: the bridge in the distance was like a toy wrapped in cotton; but the moon had risen high in the sky and as bright as a neon moon. He did not feel bad; he sat drinking and smoking through his long holder and discoursing with phantom guests—intelligently, even brilliantly in those dreams—and in a way it was better than any *real* party.

But it did not last long: to sustain a fantasy requires either a very low or a very high order of intelligence; and at midnight he was dressed and on the street. He hurried to the bar where he had sent the invitation to be posted; but it was not up. He did not ask anyone about it; he stood alone and ignored in the noisy, crowded bar. There were dozens of people there who would have come, but he did not say anything to any of them. He felt frozen, in panic: *he was unknown, invisible*; and when he turned in the smoke-hanging bar, it was as if that glut of smoke were a mouth that snapped open before him—and closed behind him— as he fled onto the street.

When he was on the street, he saw that the dark Spaniard was waiting there. He was leaning against a lamp post vomiting into the gutter; and from his torn and open shirt the cross as big as a man's hand dangled, glinting in the light of the lamp. The Span- iard turned and staggered toward him, and it was then that Farley saw he was crippled: his right leg was shorter than his left, clubfooted, and it dragged cum- bersomely after him, pointed to the side. Again he walked stooped over, bent nearly double, the cross dangling and twisting from his hairy chest like the burden of an ancient flagellant.

The Spaniard lifted his hand as if in greeting, and then dropped it: it was as if that body had straight- ened, achieved a momentary, burdenless existence—

and collapsed again from the even greater burden of its freedom. The dark eyes shone in drunkenness; a razor-thin moustache gave his face the character of a degraded and broken pimp. He was a derelict: his clothes were rags.

They greeted one another in drunkenness. The Spaniard pitched forward, arms outstretched; but before he could embrace him, Farley had jumped aside. It was like some comic ballet: the dazed, drunken Spaniard still stood there, arms outstretched, as if perplexed before a capricious lover; and then he turned—slowly, steadily—facing Farley.

Farley staggered too; he came to rest with his back against the wall of a building. "You were with that fat man," he said.

"No."

"You can't trick me," Farley said. "You were."

"Sir, no."

"You drove my car away with your cross dragging. Admit it; you did."

"I mean, sir, no. Actually no, sir."

"Why don't you admit it when I ask you?" Farley said. "I saw you."

"Sir. Sir." It was an entreaty; the man's wild, dark eyes filled with tears.

"Do not be unjust to me," he said.

Farley started to walk away, but the Spaniard followed him. Farley heard the lame foot dragging painfully behind him, and he listened with cunning: when he stopped, the sound of the foot stopped too. They

95

had not gone more than a block, when they both stopped again and Farley turned and confronted the man sternly.

"Will you admit it now?" he said.

The man's head was lowered; he merely shook it sadly from side to side.

Suddenly Farley lost patience. In the still, deserted night he shouted back over half a block at the man.

"You're trying to trick me!" he shouted. "WHY ARE YOU TRYING TO TRICK ME?"

The man only continued to shake his head from side to side, and in impatience Farley turned and hurried off.

But after three blocks, he stopped. He waited, watching the stooped man approach slowly and steadily from two blocks away. When the cripple was only a few feet away, Farley spoke.

"Well, come along then, dear," he said.

Farley and the Spaniard sat drinking upon the roof.

He placed the Spaniard in one of the honored spots—the overstuffed chair—and sat at his feet on a cushion. The moon came and went in the clear, bright sky: it moved ponderously, as if hurtled, like a slow discus, from cloud to cloud.

Farley sat talking. He could hardly sit up he was so drunk, but he talked for hour on hour. The cripple just lolled drunkenly upon the chair; his head nodded and slipped and jerked up again; his glazed eyes looked out sightlessly into the lightening sky.

Now and then Farley would lean over and shake the Spaniard awake—and talk on. He asked the Spaniard, Who was God? But of course, he couldn't answer. Then he told the Spaniard of his life, of the sadness and bleakness; but the Spaniard only sat nodding and looking out with those sightless eyes into the gray light and first movements of morning.

Finally the Spaniard left; at dawn.

And with him went all of the bottles and food he could carry. Farley sat in the cushioned chair then pretending to sleep. At his feet were two crumpled paper hats—one pink, one blue—like two strange stars fallen there from the gray sky. But Farley had acquired some cunning now and he was not asleep; he sat watching as in the half-light the Spaniard moved upon the roof. He watched as the cripple pulled himself from place to place among the ruined and splintered golf course. His leg dragged, scraping the gravel; and the broken, rotting and rusted pieces of the golf course rose up around him like flowers in a cinema garden. The cripple moved stooping to pick up bottles and plates of food; he might have been a wanderer plundering flowers in that time-forgotten garden.

Finally he left: Farley watched him as he moved with his burden to the stairs and down them onto the street.

Which became the beginning of a strange dream during the next five days. Farley remained on the roof, drinking and eating the food that was left. He drank, then slept for a while, then drank again; and those five days were like one day—one long, continuous day—with the moon and the sun each rising and falling in turn like two huge slow balls flung down and bounced from sight again and again.

And each of those five days the Spaniard returned. He came up the stairs, took his plunder of bottles and food and left.

And each time, Farley heard him before he appeared and went to the chair and feigned sleep.

They never spoke again, and when the cripple saw that he came and went unchallenged, he seemed to change there before Farley's eyes; he seemed to straighten up somewhat, and was even arrogant and a little contemptuous of Farley. During those days Farley waited impatiently the coming of the Spaniard: more and more, each of those days were centered around the moment when he would hear the opening of the door below, and the sound of that foot dragging and thumping upon the steps; and at last the dark head appeared, hairy chest exposed, the cross glinting; then he would crawl up onto the roof and make his rounds again among the remains of the golf course.

Most of the food began to rot on the third day, and the cripple disdained this and took only the bottles. He came drunk then each time—arrogant and silent except for the constant dragging of that foot. It was what Farley wanted: he sat breathless with excitement before the growing contempt of the dark man:

it took all he could do to remain silent and still in the chair. And he trembled and remembered their long talk, the black night in which he had knelt at last himself.

So that now he went in the blazing noon. It was over; the dark man would not return. It was all gone —the party scattered, blown—the last moon had plummeted, the last sun hurtled off.

He got up in blazing noon in that final devastation —the party rotting and scattered among the fallen remains of the golf course: paper hats lay crumpled, a rain of fallen stars, and white plates like cold moons.

He staggered off at last, still drunk, haggard. He had five days' growth of beard; he had not bathed or taken off his clothes in all that time, and he could smell and feel the oily oozing of liquid between his loins and armpits as he walked, and see the dirt caked upon his hands and arms. His hair was matted with sweat, and his eyes as mad as that Spaniard's had been.

Somewhere lingering about his mind was the impulse: the money was nearly gone and he must find a job. He staggered into the apartment and dressed. His hands shook so that he could hardly manage it, but when he was done he was dressed in the best of his clothes; except that his hair was still wild and uncombed, his beard still unshaven and his body still unbathed and smelling.

The girl watched from the corners; she was like a

curious animal before another, unfamiliar one. He did not seem to see her, he was that drunk and dazed; and when he came finally onto the noon street it was without a word to her.

On that street, people came and went from lunch to offices; and no disreputable, tattered and stumbling drunk could have elicited such stares and comments; for he was obviously mad, *but dressed as if he did not know he was a madman.* He staggered and stumbled and tossed his head as if trying to fling off like sequins the glazed eyes; and yet his suit was pressed, his white shirt spotless—and upon his head, set squarely and pushed down far onto his jutting ears, was the gray Panama hat.

He walked in the bleached and lucent noon. He walked, but it was as if he ran, for there was that frenzy, that hysteria: it was, in a very real sense, as if he had been shot hurtling from a cannon—arms and legs flailing and head bobbing as if jerked by wire, and propelled far beyond need and desire. He crossed and re-crossed streets a dozen times in each block, entered buildings and stores, and left again the moment he had entered without so much as a word to those who met him; went into a restaurant, sat down at the counter, and got up again and left before the waitress could approach him; went into an office building and up on the elevator as far as it went—and down again.

It was dream, madness: he felt there was something rising in him—a scream that he could not still and yet he could not give a voice to. He was running, but he was not certain where, or for what reason. He stopped once before a building and collected himself. It was a conscious effort, and in the one moment of clarity he gathered the thought: *I will get a job;* but the moment he moved forward, he was lost from it again. It was as if he were some comic character actor—sober and respectable one minute, and then going upon the stage and into his act of the incoherent drunk; but it was neither comic nor an act. And with feverish haste—as if he knew very well where he was going and what he was about to do—he rushed into the building and onto the elevator and got off at the first stop.

The hall was long and deserted and he staggered weaving to the very end of it, where he stood for a moment facing the bare wall; then lurched around and staggered back to where he had started.

He might have gone on like that for minutes, or walked up the stairs to another floor, but suddenly he stood facing a wall near a door and an imperious, inviolate brass nameplate. He stood with his nose only inches away from it: if someone had seen him, he would have thought him an unfortunate near-blind person attempting to read the name; for he stood bent close and blinking at it a few seconds—Benson Linoleum—and then turned and without a thought went through the door.

The outer office was almost bare, funereal: subdued

dinner music played from a loudspeaker, and water dripped steadily into a small fountain built into a wall. Along one wall were chairs with arm rests of the kind used in schoolrooms—only larger, highly polished and expensive—and in them sat three erect men stiff as dummies and with briefcases held exactly alike upon their laps—as if they felt somehow that if they were released they would rise up suddenly like balloons out of reach.

He stood blinking a moment at the stillness, the unobtrusive filtered light. Behind a large desk sat the receptionist—imperious too so that she looked huge there, dwarfing the men who sat lifeless in their schoolboy chairs. She wore a peasant blouse with large puffed-out sleeves like balloons, and behind her, in cases, and in cases too along all the walls, were displays of linoleum—hundreds and hundreds of squares and oblongs and circles and rectangles of linoleum, so that for a moment, with those balloon-like sleeves, she seemed to be suspended there, hovering among an exploded giant jigsaw puzzle.

The three men turned toward him—together—as if a wire connecting their jaws had been suddenly yanked; and then back.

"Well?"

The receptionist spoke over what seemed a long distance across the linoleum room. Those balloon-like arms billowed above the desk, alive.

He moved suddenly forward toward her. In that weightless, exploded room he staggered more than before: he moved like an ape—half bent over as if to grasp the floor for support, and swaying from side to side. He tried to look up, to smile at the woman as he approached, but the smile must have been hideous in that senseless face, for suddenly she stood up in horror.

Her voice nearly squeaked then, throwing up its authority:

"What do you want?"

Farley stood before her, watching curiously, fascinated as she hovered there. He was tempted for a moment to reach out and place his hands upon her shoulders and press her back to earth, but the moment he did reach out she screamed.

"Get away!"

He stood there, looking up at her and trying to smile.

She made an ugly face, waving her arms at him. "Get away now. Go on. Shoo."

The arms waved quickly, picking invisible flowers from the air before her face.

When she started to come around the desk toward him, he moved back. He tried to speak, but he could not; he could only retreat step by step as she waved him off, until at last he was in the hall again and the door had slammed in his face.

He staggered down the stairs out of the building and back onto those bright noon streets.

Only it was not noon then: the people were leaving the buildings for home.

In a little while the streets began to turn gray; with darkness some sort of sanity returned to him.

When he got back to the house, he climbed again to the roof and sat waiting for the moon to appear.

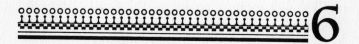

6

For Farley, during those next days, the world had become the roof. He felt secure there; it was a haven. He could look out over the white-topped houses, the toy bridge; and there was no man, no living being in his domain. There was that perfect, sculpted world only, predictable and unchanging, that he could see.

He brought up more of his possessions then—those that were important to him: he sat in his robe in the lion's-paw chair; and he lived a life that was, then, satisfactory to him in that there was only a minimum of obtrusive reality.

Like the movies before, he fed upon images; he lived entirely within them—soft, visceral misericordes which fed him. Now, in that flagrant imagination which until then had been so rigidly contained, he was one of the Great Men; each picture was a personification: the Scholar, the Great Scientist, the Explorer, the Lover, the Dashing Soldier . . . mordant, contorted.

Again the moons and suns rose and fell; the day

105

sky burst and bled, and then faded; and the inkblack night sky succeeded it: he hid in it.

Frequently the images were carnal; he acceded at last, fully, to that contained lust. In image, Lenore and the Prophet rooted in passion; the three conjoined: voluptuous, secret; and at the end of each he would hurry to a dark corner of roof and release himself. Time and again, insanely, as if the fever were inexhaustible and came flooding out at last defying past continence.

As each night descended, he would lie exhausted.

Twice, however, he came down from the roof. He would walk the long blocks to Aquatic Park and stand on a rock before the Buena Vista—always in the early evenings, when people had deserted the park for homes and dinners. He was usually alone, upon a rock against the gray sky and Bay. Not too far out, rocks clustered—sharp, angular rocks mostly; here and there washed round ones which suggested a race of giants standing there, submerged.

Farley had heard once, in one of the bars, someone telling of the seagulls at that beach—how one could go to the land's end and watch them in intercourse; and Farley had gone once, and spent nearly all of an afternoon watching; but he had not seen one pair of seagulls mating.

Now, these early evenings, one could see him looking out again. But he expected nothing; he knew he would not see them. His face then would have on it an expression of contempt as he watched the birds winging slowly above, or diving, long wings outstretched, onto the mass of rocks. His teeth would be bared in a sneer: that look proclaimed something of vast, knowing and self-satisfied scorn of those birds.

After a while, he would get down from the rock and walk in the long lengthening gray back to the roof.

During that time there was but one persistent intrusion: a dream risen from what he had thought of as the long-forgotten marshlands of childhood. Farley had thought he had buried his childhood; he had fled it; but like the gases of that marshland home, it had risen.

Now in the dream he saw his father: shop-owner, prurient: in that minator-dark south *he* raged. He was all red: lean, tall, like a bronzed cicada. Remembered vividly: the baked parchment of skin that was his neck. Prussian: hair pasted to his plateau head; an invisible monocle clamped before one eye; but with that deciduous drawl that is the southerner's concomitant passion.

The Negro, his helper, was named Moloch—a giant, black as night, suppliant and immobile both: a majestic body to belie that slow, meek spirit. . . . In the dream, revisiting, Farley watched as the red-faced man prodded the black one with a long rake-handle onto the dust-heavy street outside the store.

A cricket chirped, biting the air; the dust rose like clock-springs behind old-model cars.

What offense had been committed he never knew. The children of the town had discovered long before the Negro's gentleness; they would play with the witless giant. They would make him sit, and, grouped round him, dress him in the borrowed or cast-off clothes of the women of the town. The black man would grin happily, teeth and eyes flashing in the black face, as the children fitted over him a gingham dress, an apron; perched some bonnet upon his large head: upon his crooked arm once, a crimson purse. . . . Now the huge, lumbering Negro retreated upon the dusty street: again and again the handle came down with soft thuds upon his body. And although his arms were raised and his face full of terror and confusion, not a sound came from him; no word was spoken by either of them.

Farley saw his father's face: it was more red still with fury, a fury he had never seen there before: ecstatic; and Farley too was ecstatic, excited as he had never been before by that slow pantomime.

Finally the Negro lay crumpled upon the road. Here the dream would diffuse, it would spread out, a flower of blood: before those countless blows, the giant body would begin to dissolve. He would hear bones splintering with each blow; the skull had cracked, and rich blood was spurting forth. Now he could see the face distinctively, cast in horror: the eyes bulged with disbelief; the mouth, incredibly, opened horribly wide, stretched wider still, long teeth thrust forward. . . . Now the body was no more than a husk: it leaked blood like fountains from a dozen places; the head had fallen off, lolling wildly; and upon the sore of groin a torrent of blood burst forth.

Time and again Farley would awaken sweating from that dream; he would lean forward quickly, hoping to loose all of it onto the roof.

Awakening again from it, Farley sat trembling. The night was chill; a wind swept over him; but in the sky the moon was full: burnt orange. He sat for a moment avid, listening: he was certain some voice had called, some signal upon the purlieus of dream.

In one of Farley's more luxurious dreams, he had at last communicated with the Spaniard. They had sat as they had that night upon the roof; only then Farley had spoken with a gift that was nearly magical. He had told the Spaniard the Great Truth. But what that truth was, he did not know; he had awakened, as always, before it was revealed to him.

He got up from the chair and went to the roof's edge. He stood breathing heavily in deep, long gulps: he had begun now to experience frequent trouble in breathing. His hand shook, so he leaned upon the edge of roof, looking out.

A mist was rising from the Bay; it rose like puffs of breath from between the houses. Below, down the three flights, was a small courtyard, lit by moonlight. He had not noticed it before, and now he looked curiously. Enclosed on four sides, the building that faced it from the street might once have been a church: two ornate spires rose from it. In the courtyard itself, just below Farley, stood a white statue of Christ, half life-size, arms uplifted to him. Enclosing it, as if the owners feared its fleeing them, was a low iron piked fence.

Farley shivered and drew back from the edge. His face became suddenly very tense and excited, and he began pacing the roof, walking around it. Now and then Farley would do this in agitation; stop for a moment as if caught by a giant thought; and then, to wear down the edge of hysteria that now always threatened him, pace the roof again in long, quick strides.

If one saw him then, one would think him with an invisible, voluble companion; for as he walked, he spoke hurriedly, as if engaged actually in argument with him.

He was talking to the Spaniard.

But the words were not those of the dream; there was no eloquence to them. It was instead a kind of raging lament, a tearing. It was a supplication too, in that he pleaded to loose the words, to bring forth that Great Truth that in the dreams was given wordless utterance.

Instead, it was like a growling, the awful hunger of a beast.

At last Farley collapsed back onto the chair. His body was draped over it, folded; his hands hung loosely, and his head drooped onto his chest, as the Spaniard had sat during that night.

The dreams had failed: they had turned into the

horror of that other dream; and out of his long night of passion what was left was the void.

Suddenly Farley leaped upright upon the roof. Again he was trembling, but now from expectation. He threw off the robe, turned and made his way toward the stairs. He stood for a moment blinking against the unaccustomed light from inside the building; then he lunged down the stairs to the apartment.

Lenore was seated in the middle of the floor sorting clothes out of the bundles she had collected. She still wore the sneakers, but now the smock was gone: in its place, a long, black satin dress at least three sizes too large for her. It was a very old dress, such as one might associate with the 1890s: the sleeves came down over her hands, hiding them; the pearl buttons were closed to her chin; and, even sitting, one could see that it would trail long behind her in a train.

But Farley did not notice this; he barely noticed the girl herself. She looked up slowly as he entered, those large eyes larger still, and dark with mistrust. Again Farley appeared to her that madman; he was more dirty still from his further days upon the roof. His hair, unbarbered for so long, curled down far over his ears and neck; and his eyes had that wide, glazed and imperative look she had come now to associate entirely with him.

"What do you want now?" she asked. She hugged some of the old clothes to her breast, as if fearing he might snatch them away.

But he did not answer.

He roamed the room for some time, eyes moving quickly from place to place, almost desperately; seeking. At last he turned to her and seemed to see her for the first time.

"What are you doing?" he said. "You're always *doing* something. How is it *you* always have something to do?"

"I'm going to take a trip," she said. "I'm planning it."

"They're *rags*," he said venomously, kicking at some of them.

"If you want to see rags, there are rags," she said, glowering.

He stooped so low he was looking into her large eyes with his own.

"*You're* the smarty," he said. "All the time *you've* been the smarty."

Then without another word, he went out into the night.

He was seeking the Spaniard.

So now he loped the late dark streets—he moved in the side streets, the unpeopled places, the empty lots and alleyways and rears of houses where, incongruously, he thought to find him.

Now and then he would come upon someone; they would stare at him, and he would lope on, oblivious. A dog set up a howl lost somewhere in a crease of night; a drunkard passed by, intoning and oblivious too. When Farley would reach an area of light, one of the peopled streets, he would move off; he would seek again the darkness which, he knew, housed somewhere the Spaniard. He sought the glinting cross, the twisted walk.

But there was no Spaniard; anywhere.

After several hours, the loping ceased; Farley dragged himself upon the streets for perhaps an hour more; and then he stopped.

He was standing in the middle of a large vacant lot. To his right were some half-demolished buildings. Stoned, broken windows gaped in moonlight; upon the wall of one building, the zigzag signature of demolished, forgotten stairways; and on the top story of another a door stood opened onto nothingness.

But persistence was perhaps Farley's dominant virtue; he might have gone on yet after a moment's breath had he not seen the other figure stumbling across the lot in his direction. Even at that distance, the familiarity of that walk brought Farley up; he straightened, tensed: if he had had antennae, they would have been probing.

The figure lurched as it approached, but more in drunkenness than haste. In its arms, for the moonlight shone unobstructed there, it seemed to be clutching some loose object. The object had arms, or appeared to have arms; what looked to be legs flapped loosely around him, straddling him; but the main part of it, as if hugged dearly, was clutched to him.

As he came nearer to Farley, a white head appeared, stunted above the other, dark one. Then he saw it was the turban, and in a moment the huge body of the Prophet was swaying before him, perhaps even more surprised than he, for he stood squinting a moment, as if trying to bring Farley into view.

"What you want, white boy?" he said.

Farley did not answer; he took several slow steps backwards, cautiously. Farley saw now that what the Prophet held was a bundle of clothes, probably his own; and probably all of his possessions. What he had seen flapping were the trousers and coat of a suit; and now, in the moonlight, he looked closely, for it was a suit such as he had never seen—one of those zoot suits so common during the war. From it, a watch chain would loop to his ankle; the pants were tightly pegged, the shoulders of the coat immensely padded and wide, the lapels large and pointed like arrows; the coat itself, he could see, would fall to below his knees. Farley had heard and read of similarly dressed men lounging like cruciforms along northern streets: they had ivory women, rouged and slim as reeds upon high, piked heels . . . now here was one displaced in this western city; homeless too.

Suddenly the large man lunged forward, perhaps to pass Farley; but so intently had Farley been studying the suit, so emphatic had been the image of those northern streets, that he was startled; he drew quickly back.

The Negro again moved forward; again Farley drew quickly away.

"Wha's wrong with you, man?"

Farley just stared; he might have lifted his hands in a prayer of thankfulness had he been able.

Instead, he said, "I know you."

The small eyes came forward and focused on him.

"Yeah," he said at last. "I know you know me. I seen you watching all them times. You with that little chick."

"Will you talk with me?" Farley said.

He regarded Farley for nearly a minute, then he shook his head as if in amazement.

"Talking ain't what you need," he said.

But, unexpectedly, he reached out and put his arm around Farley.

"You buy some wine?" he asked after a minute.

Farley nodded.

"Good. You spring for some wine, and we go drink in my new house. My old lady gone off . . . but I got other friends now."

He led Farley off, back across the large vacant lot, where at the edge of the wasteland a large, red neon sign blinked on and off:

LIQUORS

Farley went through the half-broken door before the Prophet into the big room. For a moment he mistrusted his eyes, and then he looked again: the people were nearly all seated upon ledges. It was as if they had entered some gray and unlighted half-demolished store, a toy store perhaps, with life-size dolls still perched upon broken counters; only these people were real; they moved about him even now, but nearly as still as toys; and Farley had the image of going round to each one, reaching behind and winding them like mechanical toys; then seeing them whir suddenly to life and move about.

The Prophet had taken him to one of the broken buildings facing off the lot: they stood there like relics, but without the authority of history. In this one large room several ceilings and walls were torn down; plaster and debris lay scattered everywhere: the room rose unobstructed to the roof. Even here, large rents sent moonlight streaming through: the ledges were those sections of ceilings still intact. A broken cement staircase ran up nearly the entire length of it, giving the occupants access to the floors.

Each person seemed to have his own candle upon his ledge; a few candles winked slowly above him in drafts; and upon some ledges Farley saw pallets of newspapers or rags or whatever probably could be scavenged for the purpose of sleep. Now a few of the occupants leaned over curiously to see the two men: one bald head rose like an imperfect moon; then withdrew slowly, the moon waning.

More faces peered out; others withdrew.

The Prophet spoke over his shoulder as he led Farley to the middle of the room.

"This is my collection," he said. "I got me a collection here."

He waved his arm aloft at the others, who immediately all disappeared.

The Prophet kicked clear a space among the debris; what was left was smashed plaster and shards of glass and pieces of wood and the calligraphy of squashed cigarette butts.

They sat down among this beside another lighted candle and opened the gallon bottle of wine Farley had bought. With the sound of the wine being drunk by the two men, the heads and bodies began to appear again. They wanted to join them, Farley knew, but the Prophet did not notice, or was aloof and disdainful of them. They seemed to fear him; they hung back, perhaps not daring to approach.

"Where is the blonde whore?" Farley asked suddenly.

The Prophet looked at him coldly a moment. The tiny eyes attempted concentration, as if to see into him; but they were not equal to the task, and moved finally away.

"She gone," he said at last. "Nothing but white-ass trash anyhow. I beat on her a little though before she left. She had the itch to be treated like a nigger, I treated her like one."

Farley shivered. He did not know whether it was the night—the wind coming through the cracks and tears in the building—or not; and then he looked more closely at the big man.

He was no longer affluent: the flight of the blonde woman had probably left him destitute; and now, because of his violence, he was probably not wanted in any of the bars, some of which he had been excluded from long before. His shirt was frayed, unwashed; his suit was wrinkled and dirty; and he saw a pallet, higher and more luxurious than the rest, in a corner of the room. This was probably his home now, among these people: an outcast among the winos and cripples and beggars of the city.

Slowly, almost imperceptibly, some of the people had begun to emerge: like chess men, they had shifted positions about the large room, drawing nearer. One sat now upon the steps just above them—a wrinkled, yellowed man; a young, tiny man who might have been a midget or a dwarf slid down to take his place upon the ledge just over their heads; and a fat woman in shadows sat farther down upon the stairs.

It was chilly in the big room: the wind wove through its cracks, and through the high eye-like rents in the ceiling. Already they had finished nearly half the gallon of wine. The Prophet had drunk most of it, offering Farley some when he was reminded of it. Farley, like the others who crouched and perched around them in the darkness, was in awe of the huge man. It was not just his size, or even the ferocity that was evident in him; perhaps it was the solemnity: he was grimly outstaring now the eye-flame of the candle; or some tortured, twisted thing in him that was responded to by others, less flagrantly twisted. Whatever the reason, Farley sat now almost breathless, thrilling to a communicative silence he had never before experienced with another person. The wine warmed Farley, although he was not quite drunk; and even those, in shadow, slightly inhuman shapes, did not bother him.

At last Farley said, "I would like to give you some money."

The man did not answer. Again he observed Farley silently.

Farley caught his breath, hesitated a moment, and plunged forward: "You see, I thought money was the Answer."

"You was right," the Prophet said, and yawned.

Farley took the bottle and drank deeply. He sat gasping a moment, his mouth hanging open from the large draught, his eyes watering and brightening.

Finally the Prophet said, "You give me all the money you want, white boy."

"I would like to *do* something for you," Farley pursued. "You see, I need you."

"You need *something*," the Prophet conceded; then he thought; then he said, "You know what I *always* wanted?"

"What?"

"A leopard." He thought a moment, brightened. "*Yeah*. I seen one once on a chick in the Come on Inn Motel outside Memphis. Man, she had this leopard tattooed right on her belly. This thing snarled down at her crotch, and it was *fierce*; and when you look real close you see one a them mother's eyes was painted *right over her belly button*."

He sat dreamily a moment, mouth open. "I used to turn on the light and just tell her to lay there and I'd study that mean bastard. I mean, I'd *really* look at it. I think I'd know what every part of it looks like even now."

The Prophet lifted the bottle and drank for a full minute. He stood up and swung his arms wide at the room.

"*Yeah*, man, a tattoo. *I'd get me a motherin tattoo.*"

And immediately, like animals flushed, in the rush of his voice, the others retreated and scattered back to their ledges, leaving the two men alone before their candle, and silent.

The downtown streets of San Francisco after midnight are another world: here mammoth whores preside; shrivelled men lay packed hacking in dank cubicles of ancient hotels (at the end of each hallway is one small bulb . . . the color of flesh). Along the five or six streets that comprise this section it is all noise and activity: jukeboxes blare quaint euphemisms: Bing Crosby; and along the streets and in the sawdust bars men and women alike are limbless, or impaired: a giantess of a woman sports an embroidered black patch over her gouged socket; phthisistic beggars reach out with cringing servility their smooth, handless arms; ectromelians with other, tiny arms, the size of children's. Here legless men glide on crutches like stiff, folded wings: few among them are untouched.

In each of the restaurant windows signs can be seen: MEAL TICKETS ACCEPTED HERE; for those tickets issued to all the needy are accepted by the local merchants at half their value for wine, or two-thirds of their value for actual meals.

What better place to have one, solitary shop devoted to the embellishment and glorification of the human body?

For this is where the Prophet took Farley.

The two came upon this street—not spiritual strangers surely either one, but to the Prophet, perhaps, only a world less alien because these were the fallen white. . . . The two came—the one with his tense body; hunched over as if companion only to himself; and the other, huge and lumbering.

Farley had purchased another bottle along the way—Guckenheimer's 86 proof—and the Prophet drank from it.

As they came, others hurried on before them. Now and then one of them would shuffle from doorway to doorway in great heavy coats, tilting like sailboats. A rouged whore of perhaps fifty stood fixed to one gray building like a gargoyle.

They came to a small shop squat among the taller buildings. A wooden sign above the door announced: DR. HORNMUELLER'S TATTOO PARLOR; a smaller one: SPECIAL PRICES FOR GROUPS. Through this door the two men passed.

It was, in fact, no parlor at all; a gray little room separated from the other part by a curtain. There were two rickety chairs, a small table with a single ashtray, a stuffed owl, old and dust-laden, upon a shelf: its eyes were dead bulbs. Around the walls, covering nearly all the space, were drawings of tattoos: all of the obvious, the rhetorical, the boisterously sentimental affirmations and lamentations and importunings; the surrogate passions. Among these an occasional battleship, pointedly nameless; and, as if spread and foraging, wild beasts—lions and elephants and panthers and eagles and pythons; but curiously static; arrested in fury.

Although a bell had tinkled behind them from the door, for a moment they stood in silence; no one appeared. And then Farley looked, and the owl's eyes had lighted up: they were red bulbs that now blinked slowly, regularly, on and off.

On that signal, the curtains parted and what was obviously Dr. Hornmueller appeared.

Farley's first impression was of the glasses: they were large gold-metal-framed glasses, perhaps one and a half the size of normal glasses; and they gave the eyes and the face an almost elephantine look.

He was a short but powerful-looking man of about fifty with a long, pimpled nose; his face long too and oval, with heavy, drooping jowls, the skin dark and hide-like with deep, coarse creases. The hands were short and very wide upon powerful wrists, the nails broad and the color of blemished ivory.

He came toward them with curiously mincing steps for so heavy a man. He looked up at the Prophet from behind those round, huge glasses, his eyes strangely laconic.

"Yah?"

The guttural, Germanic voice too was unsettling to Farley. He turned away and found himself looking directly into the steadily blinking red eyes of the stuffed owl: from that dusty body, they seemed to peer into Farley.

"You got some leopards?" the Prophet asked.

"Ah yes. What you want, we have. We create what you desire." On sibilants, a slight hissing sound, as if there were space between his teeth.

"I want me a leopard," the Prophet said. "I'll tell you how it looks."

"You come here," the man said, and he parted the curtains and the two followed him into the other part of the room.

Here there was a sink, a small couch, long professional chair and a stool. On the table was the electric needle in its case, bottles filled probably with dyes, and the other apparatus of the artist.

The room was damp; he could smell soiled linen somewhere; and when he looked, he saw in a frame what appeared to be a diploma, or license; but hung so far up on the wall that no one could have possibly read it.

The floorboards creaked as the man walked to the table. He stood with his back to Farley now so that Farley had a full view of his large-buttocked behind. The man's trousers were too large for him. Bunched up heavily in the back, they were also too short: they came only to just above his ankles; and upon what Farley saw now were incredibly tiny feet, delicately formed, were slim red pointed shoes with large bows upon the insteps.

Now Dr. Hornmueller was making a sketch from the Prophet's description, the crayons diminished in his broad hand. Sparse white hair lifted high over his head.

The doctor worked swiftly: the crayons raced upon the page a moment; stopped; and then, at further instructions from the Prophet, raced on again.

Pretending to inspect the room, Farley moved around it on tip-toe so as to see the sketch as it progressed; but coming in front of them at last, he saw instead the German's suddenly uplifted and furious face. The glasses blinked in the light: separate eyes; the glacial expression of those real eyes was one of command and contempt: an artist was at work; and Farley froze.

He stood commanded to the spot. Again the crayons moved on; the two were head to head in what seemed some nascent passion. Now and then the doctor would stop and look up at the Prophet.

"Is good, *nicht wahr?*"

And then: "*Wunderbar, wunderbar!*"

It was obviously finished.

The Prophet sat in the big, low chair; the doctor was on the stool before him, preparing his instruments. Farley was still as if frozen as the Prophet unbuttoned his graying, frayed shirt, undid his belt and unzipped his fly: the white hair around his breasts and shoulders was like fine-spun cotton; and, below, the immensely rich black hairs of his crotch. The Prophet himself sat dazed—whether at last from the drink or not Farley could not tell, but his mouth hung open, exposing large, pink gums.

At last the doctor leaned over. His face was pressed up close to his subject, like a myopic with those huge glasses; and then Farley detected the strong smell of alcohol and saw the man quickly, but deftly, daubing that part of the Prophet with a cotton swab. Suddenly the Prophet shivered and twisted. Farley could feel the chilling alcohol on his own body too.

He looked on fascinated. The cleansing continued: it might have been an ablution; it was indeed a rite to the doctor. When the doctor had finished, he leaned forward again. Now he was sketching upon the belly of the reclining man—swiftly; but so lightly, Farley could barely see the outline. A moment later Farley heard the sound of the motor: the needle was ready.

At the first touch of it, the Prophet's body stiffened and pushed forward. He lay stretched out full length in the chair. As the needle hummed, now and then he would writhe and jerk forward; then with the subsiding of the needle, he would relax. His eyes bulged now, white globes, as if swollen suddenly in his head; sweat poured down his face in streams; but the doctor, long nose and glasses pressed close to him, held back the giant with one thick hand.

The one hand seemed sufficient; the Prophet writhed uselessly beneath it at each onslaught of the needle: the wide, ivory-colored and nearly square nails were buried in the dark flesh.

After a while, Farley began to see the colors emerg-

125

ing: little pinpricks like small, distant fires growing in the Prophet's flesh. They built slowly, the first ones larger now, the last just barely visible; spreading. At last, a few converged; then more; until one thin wavering line appeared; and then another; and still another; until after a while, Farley's gaze fastened to that body, whole areas could be seen, thin and wavering but distinct; and those less distinct growing so: an insubstantial skeleton emerging, some reverse-death.

The Prophet was no longer writhing. He sat way back, eyes bulging and sweat still clearly flowing on his dark skin; but now and then he would bring up the bottle and drink from it, his eyes lifted to the ceiling. His face had taken on a chalky pallor, drained.

Now and then the needle would stop, and the doctor would daub at the wounds from another bottle—dark, perhaps iodine—and the Prophet would wince. Farley could see the muscles working furiously in his jaws and forehead; until the doctor resumed; and he would jerk up again.

Slowly the needle progressed. So intense was Farley's concentration upon it, it was as if he could feel each tiny and pulsing pinprick; as if that pain coursed through *his* body too.

At last it was over; the bandages had been applied; and the Prophet lay, his clothes done up, full length upon the couch. He drank from the bottle again and again; his eyes were more normal now; but not a word came from him. Finally, as the last drop had been

126

drunk from the bottle, his head tilted back; the eyes closed in a tortured sleep.

Farley stood still a long time after that: he had not moved from the spot. The doctor was washing his hands at a small basin; his broad back was immense; and when he turned, drying his hands upon a violet towel, those glasses seemed even more huge; but behind them there was a kind of mocking wisdom.

Without a word to the man, Farley went to the chair and sat down on it, replacing the Prophet. He opened his shirt and trousers and lay spread out, his own flesh offered up to him.

When they came out upon the street, it was turning cold; the winter had begun, and there was a chill in the air. Now, in the early morning, the lights had died along the street; the noises had subsided. Some crippled beggars upon crutches glided swiftly in shadows; others could be seen settled in doorways, hunched down and only heads showing, like clusters of gnomes. But in all, the street was subdued: it had conceded at last its craving for death to the little death.

The Prophet was subdued too; he yawned; he was almost sober.

"It's cold," Farley said.

"Yeah."

But Farley was happy: his body was alive with what it contained. He probed the spot surreptitiously, tenderly, with his fingers; felt the edges of the bandages;

prodded the dull ache of it: something was alive and growing in him. He folded his arms across his chest— to a passerby, hugging himself from the cold—but in reality enclosing the throbbing warmth of that new containment.

They came to a corner where the Prophet would have turned off toward the old, broken building in which he now lived. Each stood a moment, as if uncertain—facing each other with, at least for Farley, a new, vast knowledge.

Then, without a word, Farley leading, they made their way back to the apartment.

7

When Farley saw within the next week that the Prophet had come to stay (had probably planned that from the beginning), at first he was alarmed; then he acceded: he picked up the belongings the Prophet the next afternoon had brought to the house and thrown upon the floor beside the mattress where he now slept and put them away carefully himself.

On the third day after his arrival, Farley began to walk with slow, heavy, weary steps, as if carrying a burden; his face was constantly flushed. He took to preparing meals for the man; he bought three tiny pastel-colored aprons he wore while serving them to him. The Prophet did not know it, but now, for a while, he wore beneath his clothes a pair of heart-shaped woman's panties he had found among Lenore's orange crates. At night, on his own mattress in the other room, he would lie sighing, naked except for the panties: he seemed to be speaking lovingly to someone there, although alone; and then, one morning, he got up hurriedly, left the house and returned within an hour with something in a brown paper bag.

When he entered his room, this time he pushed the bureau before the door. When he opened the bag, it contained a costume wig with long, golden curls.

That night Farley could be heard again in the room: soon, he stood in the panties, the curly, golden wig on his head. He had bought a fifth of whiskey; the door was blocked; and for hours he paraded about the room, the curls bouncing behind, naked except for the panties. He pranced then; he assumed poses that were both coy and dainty. Hands on hips, one finger pointed delicately now and then, he circled the room. He stood posed a moment as before an anxious lover; then he pranced on, as if enticing that lover to follow.

And finally, toward midnight, his voice, changed now and rising shrill as a bird's, could be heard singing:

"I love you a bushel and a peck, a bushel and a peck and a hug around the neck, a barrel and a heap, and I'm talking in my sleep about you, about *you-u-u-u.* . . ."

After a week, Farley took off the bandages and saw for the first time his leopard tattoo. After that, at odd moments, he would hurry to the bathroom. He would undress quickly and there, his thin body exposed to the mirror, view it for long periods of time. He could not see himself full length in the mirror; it was too high; so in order to see all of the leopard at once he would have to climb onto the edge of the tub. There, balancing precariously, he could see it reflected in its entirety; and not once did he fail in a sharp intake of breath at the sight of it.

At this time he had what he thought a magnificent idea: he would go back to work, acquire the money, and then return to the tattoo parlor to add to the leopard.

At first he thought of small things: a sparrow above each breast; a snake wound round his phallus; then he thought of a lion—a glorious, golden-maned lion, paws raised, snarling, down the entire length of his back. There might be an eagle upon each buttock; the long necks of giraffes would be on his arms to the wrists, their bodies one upon each shoulder; upon his legs, upside-down green crocodiles, his feet forming their heads, his toes their exposed, pointed teeth.

Standing there upon the tub, viewing his leopard, in imagination now all of his body, every inch of flesh, was covered—even to his face, which was a great wide-eyed owl, its eyes his now; asps coiled as if to strike within each ear. . . . He could see his multi-colored body even then: as he moved, each of the animals moved; as each organ functioned, each muscle contracted or expanded, those beasts would come alive, move upon him writhing great splashes of color.

Before each new acquisition of tattoo, he dreamed, there would be some secret (to him), ritualistic intimacy with the Prophet.

Now *Farley* roamed the house . . . making it more welcome for the Prophet when he returned each morning. He would prepare little meals and leave them for him, purchase small bottles of *apéritifs* that he might drink before them (the Prophet would swallow the tiny bottles whole, in one gulp); he spread one of his lavender sheets over the mattress; and even left money—not much; he had not much left—in some conspicuous place for him to find.

Several times Farley waited up for him; they talked in the late dead mornings; but of course the Prophet could not make much sense out of it. Usually of some obscure Truth Farley seemed certain of finding, of his (before) lonely passion. The Prophet would nod; he would yawn; he would ask Farley finally to fry him some pork chops; but mostly he would just drink from the bottle Farley would provide on each of those occasions, falling off finally into a noisy sleep.

Which did not really bother Farley, for he would just go on talking as if he were still awake.

Now Lenore was watching too; she was watching from corners, from obscure and unexpected places. Farley was aware of it: a cunning smile would appear when he knew she was at it.

But she had her cunning too, long practiced: she would watch from everywhere: from doorways, from behind furniture, once even from a closet.

For a while, he was certain *she* wanted the Prophet for herself; she would come one night and snatch him from him; but he was certain then of the faithfulness of the big man. *What could he see in her?*

However, after a while, the doubt became an obsession: this passion was *his*, long sought. He would not share it with her.

One night he waited until he heard her climb onto the bed; he waited an hour more; then, slowly, he opened her door.

He reached inside the door, pushed the wall switch that turned off the light; then, waiting again a few minutes, he slipped into the room, closing the door quietly behind him.

He stood first inside the doorway in almost total darkness, very still, to accustom himself to the darkness before he moved; then he did move—at first standing; then bent over to make himself smaller; and finally, upon hands and knees, crawling to the bed. He knelt there, his face perhaps inches from hers. He could hear her breathing, but not for a minute was he deceived that she was asleep: she was awake, eyes wide, he knew, and watching him.

At last, after perhaps ten minutes, he moved slowly, bare inches at a time, back to the door; and was gone.

Farley lived in this secret passion as he had never in any other before. Now he would perform unobtrusive little tasks for the Prophet: lay out his possessions; brush that outlandish but (to him) beautiful suit with artful care. He would prepare special dishes for him: cold fried chicken, which Farley would prepare and cool in the refrigerator; meatballs reeking with garlic; even once, a *pâté de foie gras* that Farley bought and the Prophet did not even touch.

However, once, about a week after the Prophet had first come to the house, he did not return one morning to sleep; he did not appear until well into the next day; and when, three days later, this was repeated, Farley was furious.

When he returned that time the next afternoon, Farley said, in a high, arch voice that would visit him sometimes now, and in an unexpectedly cold tone,

"I would appreciate it, when you intend to spend the night out, if you would inform me before. After all, one makes preparations, one makes one's own plans."

The Prophet had just stared: tiny eyes had focused hard for a second on Farley; then, reeling drunk, he had plunged down on the mattress.

When later he awoke, Farley was sitting upon Lenore's couch, watching him fiercely. He seemed almost simpering sitting there; feminine. He had been cooking fried pork chops for him; he wore one of the tiny aprons; and as he was about to lash out again against his truancy, the Prophet held up a hand.

Farley blinked, mouth open.

"What was that you said—I gotta *tell* you where I go?"

Suddenly Farley was in panic. He began twisting on the couch.

"No, no," he started to protest.

"Just wanted to be sure I was hearing right," he said.

He lay back down and closed his eyes.

Farley sat trembling. He said hysterically, in a high, shrill voice that he could not recognize as his own,

"Whoever it is you're seeing, I don't care; it doesn't matter to me. You can have all the friends you like and I won't say *one* word. You can even bring them home if you like. You could do that—I wouldn't mind. Now wouldn't that be nice?"

The Prophet opened one eye and looked at him; then closed it, and he was again asleep.

That was when they came.

At first, only one or two came to the house; those people perhaps from the broken house—as if the Prophet, actually, had announced an invitation to all those people he had before lived with upon the streets and in that old building.

For that was surely who they were: derelicts, winos, old whores (some of those upon those ledges in shadows?).

One evening four of them were there (the Prophet was not there—he still, now and then, was gone for days at a time). They came very timidly then, the men with hats in hand, the lone woman, Farley knew, primped-up and beautified as best she could for the occasion (her hair: matted, gray-unwashed, but set with tight curls at the temples like tassels; bangs

135

pasted to her forehead with spittle: a withering flush had been pinched into her cheeks); came humbly, seated at last demurely, stiffly erect, like outlandish statues, upon the couch; for, Farley knew, to them yet he was above them: his clothes were still those of a respectable man; he lived here, disreputable as it was to most, and so *he* was respectable.

The servility was not feigned, he knew: to the destitute, servility is a social concomitant; the home is to be viewed in awe, but seldom touched. Yet these were vicious people, he knew (he had seen enough by then); they lived solely through viciousness: the fact that they had survived to be sitting there then was proof of the extent to which their viciousness had been employed. For, like certain species of carnivorous fish, they would attack only the helpless, those who were vulnerable; but then they would attack with fury.

But now they sat in humility: the men looked round with bulging eyes, hardly daring to move their necks; and the woman, conscious as she would be almost to the last of the vestiges of femininity, grotesquely demure.

Farley brought them tea and what there was to eat, Lenore peeping out at them. He sat across, not knowing what to say to them. The woman, heavy, big-breasted, sucked at her teeth as she smiled primly at him; two of the men, of identical height and build, their faces covered by those masks that produce frequent, astonishing likenesses among the poor, were expressionless; void; but the third, a dwarf who sitting came only to the shoulders of the two men, wore a mauve-colored blazer and was grinning now an almost completely abandoned grin. Farley's first impression was that the little man might get up and suddenly do somersaults upon the floor: he had about him that haunted anguish of the circus dwarf.

These were the first. They were followed by others gradually over a period of weeks, all equally abject and respectful and thankful for the food and drink and warmth; and one night one slept over—the dwarf: he slept curled in a corner; and the next morning Lenore stumbled upon him suddenly, just awakening. She came upon him rubbing sleep out of his wrinkled face with chubby fists, and she made him some coffee which he sipped, shivering for a while in the morning cold. When he was done with the coffee, he sprang up quickly to his full two-and-a-half-feet height, did a loose and intentionally clumsy dance, rolled over once like a hoop and came to a stop standing on his head, his face wrinkled further with a comic expression and his tongue sticking out good-humoredly but tauntingly at her.

Lenore had been watching him from the moment she gave him the coffee; she had walked in her long-trailing dress to the farthest corner of the room, and there, upon her haunches, stared intently, fascinated, at the little man.

When he was done, he pulled from his pocket a checkered cap, fitted it low over his face in the style of a Parisian *apache*, again with a comical, self-mocking smile. Then he went to the door. He had to reach above his head to turn the knob. He bowed very low, grinning; then he was gone.

After that others began to spend the night too—none nearly as entertaining to Lenore as the dwarf, whom after that morning she seemed always to be awaiting: these were the broken ones; the discarded; but now Lenore came out of her room when the Prophet was not there. She would sit in a corner and watch them: a kind of world was evolving there where there had been no world for so long.

She even ventured a few times to serve them: still sullenly, head still lowered nearly to her chest, she would bring in the food and drink, hand round the utensils; even once serving tea in what cups they had. In that black, heavy dress that trailed at least two feet behind, she might have been an actual hostess at a tea.

But Farley did not remember the dream-hostess he had once imagined in that same room.

Now they were nearly never alone: cripples came swinging in on crutches; beggars with those pasted looks of eager supplication; frail puffs of women like dying flowers. Some drunk at that point—others expectant and eager to be drunk.

Farley would encounter them here and there: he had come upon one asleep in a closet one morning; another in the kitchen, a thin hawk of a woman, rooting with twisted fingers through the crumbs and waste of the night before, fitting bits of food quickly into the tight, round hole of her mouth, as fearing they might be stolen from her suddenly.

He was not unhappy about it. Now he too would sit watching them. It was as if a community were forming; a beggar community true, but out of his long loneliness he felt it better than no community at all: it was his rooftop party dream come true, although seen as if through a distorting lens.

But it was not right either, he knew. To them, he was only an observer; there was no real satisfaction to it: he was there, but never part of them. When he would approach one group, they would become instantly silent; an individual questioned would spout phrases, automatic as a canary; then, having performed his duty, move off to join his companions.

At last, Farley abandoned the front room; he did not go near them; but he would sit in another room dreaming of conquests of that beggar kingdom.

What was left of the money was quickly going: between what he had given the Prophet and the additional expenses of the others, not a great deal remained.

Once, about a week earlier, Farley had gone out to buy rice and beans and hamburger so that he might make a pot of food for them all. He had started out toward the usual cheap street where he now most often shopped and was known—but suddenly he had found himself swerving off.

A moment later he was on a side street; and five minutes after that he emerged onto a square in the middle of which was an immense supermarket (the name MURCHERSON's in neon letters) he had never seen before.

It was one of those monstrous conglomerates: one could buy anything, from a lawnmower to bird cages. Spielers spoke at the heads of aisles into microphones hung from harnesses around their necks, offering new breakfast foods, magic utensils. One entered upon rubber mats; doors flung open electrically then to entice entry even upon their edges. The store itself was perhaps two city blocks long.

Farley entered; bought what he had come for; but still he had lingered in a complex intimacy that might not entirely have been the result of the motivational-research psychologists and architects who had planned the store.

He walked through long rows filled high with foods; browsed touching the bright chromium of the frozen foods section; stopped finally before the stripped and naked upside-down chickens and geese and ducks upon hooks at the meat counter.

A crowd was there—mostly women—some fat with great plumes to their hats and in fur coats, like giant chickens themselves; others as skinny as one long, plucked turkey that hung lonely above their heads.

A sign said: GIGANTIC SALE; and the women were jostling one another before the counter. Elbows thrust out sharply like rapiers; abundant flesh merged, and then parted.

Farley listened carefully: he could hear the creakings of the accouterments the women wore beneath their dresses; and he could smell the commingled, sickening odors of half a dozen cheap perfumes.

He stood back from the crowd of women, leaning far forward at the waist, a distasteful expression upon his face. Quickly, as if sensing something, he looked first at the hanging, naked birds—then at the women again; and then back at the birds.

His expression was very intense. He might have detected something there that no one else had ever seen.

One woman, fatter than the others, was pushing progressively forward to the counter with her hips and stout, muscled arms. She used her large hips to force wedges in the crowd: other women were flung off them with an ease that was partly the force of that abundant flesh, but also of long experience, and the assurance that experience brings. Farley watched this woman for a long time. She too wore a hat, but on hers were cherries and oranges and other fruit, each upon little wires that bobbed and jiggled as she moved—a tiny hat that looked strange upon her mound of upswept hair, as if it were not a hat at all but some alien creature descended suddenly and watching too.

Farley shifted onto his other foot; he still leaned forward. He was peering with such fascination that he was not aware for some time that *he* was being watched; then he looked swiftly around.

It was one of the clerks—a young man of about nineteen with a face as pale and stripped as those hanging birds. He had a long, pointed nose that seemed to be smelling Farley as he had smelled the women; he wore his blue store's jacket with hauteur, a badge pinned to the breast of it; the knotted part of a pink tie peeked out from it. Somehow, he looked as if, in spite of his haughty expression, he wanted desperately to belong to the uniform; but the uniform refused to belong to *him*.

Grudgingly, Farley swung his carriage and disappeared down one of the aisles.

Farley stayed in the store an hour longer: he passed through each aisle a dozen times, marveling at the mountains of food. Now and then he would encounter another of the store's clerks in the same blue jackets and badges; he peered close once and saw that the writing on each of them was the clerk's name, and the inscription beneath, I AM HERE TO SERVE YOU; but mostly Farley hurried past them, almost slinking.

Here was a cornucopia; all the immense riches of food and bright objects—those to feed the flesh and to pamper it and to enhance it, and even those to amuse it—were contained here. They could be had by plucking them from their shelves.

A moment later, Farley had one of them in his trousers pocket—a large bar of chocolate.

The moment he knew it was there he was amazed;

he was instantly terrified. He stood eyes bulging and rigid, hands pressing tightly the handle of the cart; for he was certain, at any second, some hand would reach out and seize him, some crude face would peer into his own; but no hand came. Slowly he allowed himself to relax; he let his eyes wander around: the people went about their shopping as usual, oblivious of him.

He pushed the cart hurriedly out of that aisle, down three aisles and into the larger open space where produce was stacked in long bins.

He stood sweating then; his hands shook; but *no one had seen him.* He looked around again: a fat lady and her small husband were poking through rutabagas; an aisle over, the three young children of a dispeptic-looking couple were marauding the shelves of breakfast foods, scrambling for their favorites among the vast varieties. Then he knew: *he was invisible to them:* their greed among the immense, offered riches blinded them to *all* else.

No one had noticed. Only the officials would have cared, those who stood to lose by his theft; or those in their employ. Indeed, the huge market was designed to entice and narcoticize: the subtle lighting would have done justice to an Alexandrian brothel; Mantovani piped in softly to lull them; and the articles arranged with a symmetrical beauty that invited violation of them.

Of course, Farley had heard stories of plainclothes detectives; any of the employees would surely have apprehended him had he been seen by them; and he had heard too the rumors of motion picture cameras secreted . . . recording; guards patrolled the ceiling, peering from concealed mirrors; but if one were *clever*. . . .

He made a tour of some of the aisles. He passed the employees again, studying them this time; but none seemed to pay any particular attention to him. Then he saw, standing leaning at the head of one aisle, the arrogant young clerk with the pink bud of tie, and slowly he moved his cart toward him. This one looked around; he even sneered; but Farley guessed the sneer was habitual—he was probably a supervisor of sorts— and it was not directed at him at all.

To test it further, he went down another aisle. Here were rows of canned delicacies: Norwegian sardines, smoked salmon, bright red maraschino cherries in bottles: he stopped before the cherries. First he looked around: only one old woman picking suspiciously among jars of sauerkraut. He took down a small bottle of cherries; examined it; then covered it from sight with the palm of his hand. He made a gesture, as if returning the bottle, then brought it to his side. Walking down a few paces, with his hand between himself and the shelf, he casually eased it into his other pocket; then he walked, not too fast, but quickly, to the check-out counter.

After that, Farley went to stores where he was not known to steal what was needed.

He did not go back again to the supermarket for a

week: with the cunning now of his new identity, he knew it was dangerous to be seen too often in the same stores; he worked each of two dozen over a period of a week.

He made an itinerary: he stole a school notebook, and in his now large, laboring scrawl he listed the stores, and the days and hours he would go to them; and carrying the notebook with him, when he had finished with each, he would mark a large check beside its name. Each time he would do this upon a street—in a doorway or alley. He would take out the folded notebook and the stubby end of pencil and, taking perhaps five seconds, make his laborious check beside the name; then he would replace it and go on to the next.

In the evenings, after his rounds were done, he would take out the notebook and study it. At first, the few check marks annoyed him; he was anxious to see them strung out over all the pages. But later, when there were a great many, he would go over them joyfully: he would count each one for the day; then the total for the week; then the total for all the weeks; and then he would go back and count from the beginning again to see that he had not made a mistake.

After a while, however, he realized that the possession of the book was dangerous: if he were caught, and it found on him, it would be disastrous; and so he contented himself by hiding it under his mattress and only taking it out at night.

Farley was cautious: he had yet to learn his trade.

He might, through the Prophet, or any of the others who now came to the house, have learned it quickly; but again, it was a private thing, like his leopard.

At first he taught himself how to stand, and where, so that his actions were best hidden from others; to study the shops and the faces of the owners and employees to detect possible fanatics. Now it was cold enough to wear his large overcoat; the pockets were very deep. He sewed other pockets inside it, and he learned not to wear bulky clothing beneath so as to have more room. He learned also how to move his hand without moving any other part of his body; he spent hours before the bathroom mirror at night studying his expressions and poses. Now and then he would employ an innovation that he thought entirely his own, and of these he would be especially proud: he conceived the idea of carrying a book that he might slip flat objects unobtrusively behind until they could be transferred to his pockets; he sewed a long pocket slung inside the collar of his coat so that, appearing to put his hand to his neck, he could drop small items into it; he even practiced before the mirror staring down clerks: a lifting, arch look that he was certain conveyed an arrogant superiority.

But for all his care and work, strangely, he did not alter important things about himself: he did not wear clean clothes, although he had them; he did not take care to shave or comb that wild hair; nor could he rid his eyes of that haunted, lost look.

At first he picked up only a few things here and

there that they were in need of—food and whiskey
mostly, although little of the whiskey since that was
the most difficult: a drunk would steal where a hungry
man might not; and the bottles were always placed in
conspicuous places, in places where he was most vulnerable. And then, as his skill grew, so did his arro-
gance—he began popping things into his pockets that
were luxuries, or hardly needed at all: cheap pieces
of jewelry, a pair of rubber gloves for washing dishes,
pocket books he knew he would never read, small toys
and boxes of crayons from a five-and-dime; and, finally,
from that same counter, an object he knew was too
large, but for that reason had been a challenge to him
for days.

For that object he had taken particular care: he
had skirted the counter for three consecutive days.
He had prepared by measuring it casually one of those
days with his hand; that night he had enlarged the
long pocket inside his coat; and on the fourth day,
the salesgirl, a young, tight-mouthed girl he had
guessed correctly was more absorbed in calculating the
merits and advantages of the boys and young men in
her life, who positively glowed with avarice (on the
first day, she had judged Farley as of no interest to
her at all, and so thereafter hardly glanced at him)—
that day, when she had turned for just a moment to
study herself appreciatively in the mirror she kept
beside the cash register, Farley had swept up the long
box, inserted it into the pocket, and was already walking casually away.

147

This, his largest acquisition, he had no use for at all: it was a Monopoly set; and when he returned, he flung it onto the couch indifferently.

But once he was almost caught.

It was in a notions store that he had almost not included on his list; he had been suspicious of the owner's looks: eyes a little too intense, darting; a long face, his nose long too and running parallel down the face which he sensed was the face of a wary and tormented man; but he had included it anyway—he had no other notions store on his list—and the bright objects inside had fascinated him.

This time it was early morning; there were only two customers in the store—two portly women together—and the owner was occupied with both of them. Farley moved slowly among the counters, as he had trained himself to do, his vision taking in most of what was happening to the sides of him. One of the women breathed very heavily—an asthmatic: it sounded almost like a death rattle; the other, perhaps her sister they looked so much alike, had a concentrated expression, intractable and perverse, so that he thought the owner would be occupied with her for some time.

Going to a counter that contained religious objects, Farley stopped before a small figurine of Christ. He read the instructions on the package next to it which said that, plugged in, the eyes would light up, the eyes of the Saviour guarding you through the night. Upon it was printed the inscription: OUR SAVIOUR WATCHES OVER ME IN THE NIGHT.

This was Farley's mistake. If he had not temporarily surrendered his concentration to the bemusing thought of the Saviour watching over *him* in the night, of those eyes guarding *his* night, he would have seen the owner striding over to him as the object was lowered to his pocket.

As it was, some sixth sense saved him from total disaster (*Was* Jesus watching over him *now*, during the day?); perhaps the sound of the man approaching, or the fury he seemed to bring with him round all the store with his flat-footed walk; but at the moment he reached him, standing just slightly to the side of him, Farley had already begun to raise the figurine, and in a second it was replaced.

"What's that you was doing?" the man demanded in a loud voice.

Farley stood as if turned to stone. His mind raced furiously to bring forth one of those cutting sentences or superior or innocent expressions he had practiced so long; but none came: nothing came.

"I seen you around here snooping before," the man said, his voice lifting higher still. "Some kinda creep you ask me." This last to the two women, both of whom had drawn closer, both with lips clamped tightly shut, and the one with the fiercer expression leaning forward, as if detecting an odor about Farley.

Farley began to protest.

"Get out, get out!" The man was waving his arms now; his long face was nearly purple. In panic, Farley fled the store.

He ceased his activities for that day; he hurried in a frenzy back to the house and into the room where he had hidden the notebook beneath his mattress. For a few minutes he just sat talking wildly to himself and beating the edge of the mattress with his fists; then he got up, and, still muttering wildly, beat the walls until some of the plaster started to shake loose over him; then he went on his knees before the mattress, withdrew the notebook and pencil, turned to the page where the notions store was listed, and drew two furious lines through the name; then he slashed the pencil through it again, tearing the page.

Even so, he was not contained. He got up and stormed through the rooms, looking for what he did not know. Then, in the front room, he came upon one of the derelicts asleep upon newspapers in a corner. Farley rushed to him and kicked him as hard as he could in the buttocks; the man jumped up dazed both from sleep and pain.

"*Get out,*" he screamed at the fleeing man. "*Get out, get out, get out!*"

But that did not deter Farley for long: few things could; and the next day he was back at his rounds. At first tentatively, true; but now it was even more intense—it was as if he had found a kind of God-likeness in the thefts; an intense and genuine identity he had never known before; and the possibility of detection and punishment was even more exciting to him: the face of that shop-owner and the contemptuous expressions of the two women who had witnessed his shame seemed finally to push him on to further excesses.

He took chances now; he abandoned frequently his previous caution: he would go into a store and pick up the nearest object without even looking around; he would steal more and more outlandish and useless objects.

One cold afternoon he spent nearly an hour in front of an orthopedic shop. In the window was a legless but life-size mannequin, a pale pink color, which attempted no semblance of life-likeness: its fingers tapered to round ends; its face was a sloping globe without features; its torso nearly shapeless; and, strapped all around it, enclosing it as if in some medieval torture vest, the belts and harnesses and straps and tight girdle-like objects sold in the store.

The window was dusty; the objects and the mannequin had probably been placed there years before; and so the impression was even more lifeless than the owner's lack of art had managed to create.

But to Farley it was beautiful: the sight of that trapped and tortured thing brought from him a response that was almost tortured in himself. For was he not misshapen too? Was he not constrained and twisted and without final form? Farley nearly moaned there then before the sight of it. Mouth wide, gaping, his own anguish was voiceless too confronting it.

He had paced before that window perhaps twenty times: his frustration was almost a rage, for he knew there was no way to manage it, unless he were to break into the store at night; for an old man with long black hairs growing from both his nostrils sat just inside the doorway, stiffly twisted himself, as if he were the prisoner of his own wares, or had somehow become shaped by years of proximity to them.

Instead, at last, defeated, he went into the large supermarket and stole six items from six different shelves in a row.

At night he would return exhausted from his long travels. He would lie sleepless on his mattress, turning again and again in his impatience for the morning; and when he did sleep, dreams surged up containing all of the items he had seen and not managed to steal; and some that he had not seen at all.

Every few days he would find himself drawn again to the window of the orthopedic shop.

At this time he sometimes did not notice the other life around him: the derelicts had come in greater force. But if he thought of them at all it was only as some creature that consumed his acquisitions each day, so that he might go out the next to procure it more. It was a voracious creature, he knew. He fed it.

At the end of each day, his coat and pockets bulging with his many trophies, he would stand at last at the end of one or another row of shops. He would watch the lights go out one by one; the awnings rolled up by clerks. He would see the employees and owners emerge from the shops; and at last, in that quiet street, the doors pulled shut and locked, there would be only that long stretch of darkness, and the silence, and Farley standing alone at the head of it.

Farley had discovered an entrance to the little courtyard behind the deserted church: an alleyway led into it from the street; but blocked by a high, locked door. Farley had found that by using the doorknob as a foothold he could climb up onto the door and drop down into the alleyway; from there he would emerge onto the small courtyard beside his building, where he could sit in peace outside the fenced-off white Jesus.

Here he went one of those nights when that sadness had come over him; that feeling still of incompletion.

He felt the Prophet was deserting him: he was gone for days at a time. He would now not even allow him their long talks at night. Now and then, drunk, the Prophet would take one of the whores on his mattress for the night: some vile, filthy scarecrow of a woman; and Farley would become sick with this desecration and betrayal. His feelings of panic and rage vied with that of hatred of the man: no matter how he tried, he felt powerless to obtain his favor. He had attempted to please the Prophet by bringing him special gifts from his forays: none worked; each day he grew more indifferent to him. Those times he did acknowledge him, to Farley's shame, it was with contempt before the others.

This night he brought two fifths of whiskey, one in each of his coat pockets. He opened one and sat drinking beside the white figure, its arms uplifted to no beatific image, but to the flat, windowless side of the house, dark with shadows.

He sat hunched over in the pale moonlight, but now and then he would look up at the white face, which gleamed in it. Farley had no religion; what God could he give service to? But he felt almost peaceful there for moments at a time; he felt contained; and the figure, perhaps half the size of the real man it represented, gave him a kind of peace he seldom knew now. Once he had crawled over the fence and looked into the face: it had on it that sublime look one sees on statues of Christ. But that could not fool Farley from the hard, sculpted unreality of the stone: it was just a statue; and he had climbed back, satisfied, but suddenly depressed.

That night was the worst: he got very drunk, very quickly. He was depressed. He felt, for the first time since he had begun, unfulfilled. He fed with his labors a monster he did not love; that one he did was scornful of him.

Now he looked at the white Christ ("Christ was *black*," the Prophet had shouted when he had told him about it. "Any fool knows *that!*"), almost sneering: he hated it.

At last, staggering, the one bottle empty, he left the courtyard and went back to the rooms. No one spoke to him: four of them were seated playing the game of Monopoly; the Prophet was there, drunk, but he ignored him too. It was as if, to Farley, the moment he achieved visibility, invisibility descended again inevitably.

A fever raged in him then (Was it the cold winter chill of the courtyard?); the sight of the man now with one of the whores (nearly naked) fed his hatred and loneliness. He was alien again, excluded.

He thought for a moment that if he could do something wonderful for the Prophet, unparalleled, he might win him; but what? Staggering, he had gone back to his room, hiding the other bottle in one of the bureau drawers.

And then he remembered: it was an inspiration. He took from the closet one of his large suitcases, and nearly trembling at the sudden perfect beauty of it, his gift of love, he rushed from the house into the night.

He stood before the little shop perhaps twenty minutes. It was now late; dark night. The street fortunately was a small one: no traffic; and those passersby who occasionally came and went seemed as indifferent to him as all the others.

When he had decided, he waited only a moment longer; then he swung the suitcase crashing into the window of the orthopedic shop; scooped up the dummy and ran.

He cut quickly through a small backstreet first. Behind him, windows suddenly were lighted on the street of the theft; he could hear excited voices; a police whistle blew. But he was cautious; cunning: he moved slowly, but with assurance, from small unlighted street to unlighted street. A few blocks farther, he straddled a fence, pulling the suitcase after him, the dummy cradled in his arms: there he stooped, placing the dummy inside the suitcase; hurried then through a long alleyway; from there to yet another street, until at last he emerged onto Grant Avenue. Staggering, but almost casual, he made his way back to the house.

He opened the door and, wild-eyed, among the jeers of all of them, opened the suitcase and placed the dummy at the Prophet's feet.

The Prophet just looked at it once; kicked it aside as Farley knelt before him.

The others laughed; they jeered: *all* were drunk that night.

At last, Farley rose, went into his room. He placed the dummy before his mattress; sat for a moment looking at it with hatred; then he began to undo, very carefully so he knew how they were adjusted, the various straps and appurtenances; stripping naked, just as carefully, he fitted them to himself.

When he was done, he moved experimentally: constrained, his movements like a mechanical man's, he walked about the room, creaking.

Slowly, painfully at last, he went out of the room toward the front room.

But the lights were out; he knew they were having sex; even the Prophet with the drunken whore.

Nearly wailing with grief, creaking in his confinements, he began to move into the room; until the voice of the Prophet came out of the darkness, shocking, arresting him:

"You are *evil*, man. I mean, you are *really evil*."

Then the other voices came from the darkness, chanting it—a chorus jeering that one word.

In darkness, Farley clasped his hands to his ears. He turned; and although he wanted desperately to run, he could not. With his burden, laboriously, step by step, he moved slowly, among creakings, back to the sanctuary of his room.

That night Farley did not sleep: he sat in the darkness drinking the other bottle of whiskey.

In the morning he did not feel drunk, but he knew he must be: as slowly the room filled with light, as if spilled into it by a giant saucer, so the whiskey flowed from the bottle; at the final burst of daylight, the last drop was gone.

Unsteadily, Farley arose; he took from one of the closets his best suit, shirt, tie. He laid the shirt and tie carefully upon the mattress, and he hung the suit from a nail in the wall where once a picture had hung.

There was a bureau in the room—one of the relics of his own apartment—and rooting through the drawers, he came up with a hand mirror. In it he studied his face a moment, neither with horror nor surprise, but as if to see what part of him he had started out to be still existed; then in underwear and the shirt he still wore, he went into the bathroom through the sleeping house.

Stripping naked, he washed in cold water with his shirt. He washed every part of himself very carefully, scrubbing his skin hard with the wet shirt. He shaved after that, then poured water onto his hair, using his fingers to comb it. When he was finished, shivering in the cold house, he hurried back into the other room.

There he carefully unfolded the shirt and put it on; knotted his tie in the hand mirror; put on the suit and shoes and his large overcoat. When he was done, he knew something was still missing: he was not complete; and he stood staring hard into the mirror, as if it might be revealed magically to him there. Then it came to him and when it did his reflected mouth opened in the mirror in a smile; then stiffened at what he saw: his teeth had begun to decay now; spreading roots of blackness distorted that smile into something hideous.

Quickly, he put away the mirror and went to the closet and brought down from the shelf the remembered object: the Panama hat. It did not disturb him that it was winter; without the hat there could be no going; but when he put it on he knew instantly it was not right, and he took out the hand mirror again: in it, the hat sat very small on his head: his hair had grown now so long that the hat rode like a little vessel atop it. Making an angry face, he pushed it down as far as it would go: it fitted then to his head, but now hair sprouted out all around it, giving him an even more fierce expression. Nevertheless, it was there; he was whole.

Tip-toeing through the sleeping people, now and then having to walk over one, he made his way out into the chill morning air.

When he got to the square where the supermarket was, it was still not seven o'clock; it would not open until eight; and he stepped inside a doorway to wait. The square was nearly deserted—it was Sunday morning. A woman, her hair done up tight in brown curlers like large worms, and in a housecoat and overcoat, was walking a dog. It was a very tiny dog, a Chihuahua, and it shivered in the cold air as it trotted reluctantly beside its impatient mistress.

No one else was in sight. Now and then a car would approach slowly, as if animate and drugged in the dawn light. A few lights had gone on in windows, but everything else was still; not a sound.

Then the woman passed the doorway in which Farley stood, now more impatient, pulling the little dog behind. She pulled it after her around the corner: the dog skidded there, trying to keep up: four paws worked furiously a moment, nails screeching against the concrete; then they were both gone.

At seven-thirty the employees began to arrive— dragging and hunched over and looking dazed themselves. Finally, at a few minutes past eight, the doors opened, and Farley crossed the square and entered the store.

He was the first customer.

He went to the nearest aisle, took down a jar of olives without glancing around and put it into his pocket. He waited a moment, then moved on.

The fluorescent lights seemed fierce to him now. Shielding his eyes with his arm, he looked up at them.

For a moment, he felt dizzy; he began to stumble; then his hand went out and he steadied himself upon a pile of sardine cans: he put two of these into his pocket, then went on.

Alone in the market, it seemed even more immense to him: a giant mouth that at any moment might swallow him. Behind each of the service counters, employees waited. Far off, almost immobile, stiff in their fresh uniforms, they seemed unreal however; mannequins.

In a little while, the store stirred; it came to life. Since it was to close at noon, early-Sunday shoppers poured into it now. The clerks stirred too; but with a suggestion of contrived humanity. The refreshment stands opened: long counters with chromium appurtenances like the snouts and ears of animals imbedded into the walls: some sent up steam in great puffs, large heads rising above smaller ones.

But Farley was oblivious to all of it: he went quickly from aisle to aisle, stuffing his pockets with abandon. He walked bent forward over the carriage, as if it supported him, and peering over it at some dim, distant object. Now and then he would pass one of the clerks with their badges and blue coats. Once he even thought he saw the young clerk he had encountered the first day; he could not be certain: each one seemed identical to him.

By eleven-thirty his coat was bulging; he had in his basket a loaf of bread and a box of sugar.

For a few minutes longer he reeled down aisle after

aisle; then he was before the liquor department. To him, the long rows stretched endlessly. Looking up, he saw his reflection from above: a thin, slanting mirror ran the length of the shelves, showing the movements of all who stood before them; and reaching high, very high, he took down a fifth of Old Overholt.

He might still have gone on, but there was no longer any room: in the stuffed coat, he seemed puffed out like some malformed person: his head sat ridiculously small upon the distended body. Reeling, the room whirling about him, he pushed heavily forward, step by laborious step, the items clinking and rattling as he went.

He passed throught the check-out counter without incident; he was upon the street.

For a moment he stood blinking at the sudden glare of daylight gloom. Swollen as he was with all his acquisitions, he felt ponderous, improbable. Again he began to reel; he might have fallen, except that suddenly two arms seized him, one on each side.

"Come along quietly," a voice said. "No trouble now."

A long, shed-like place: rows of crates and cartons and sacks; a high, beamed ceiling; a desk before which a stout man sat: the hands had gone, winging off like birds: he looked up a moment, as if expecting to see them circling there beneath the high ceiling; then, staggering, back.

Beside him, a pink bud of tie; pale face like a plucked bird's; but smiling.

"Empty 'em," the voice behind the desk commanded.

Slowly, he unloaded the coat of its possessions onto the desk; he took it off and emptied the inside pockets. At last, finished, there was a long, low whistle of astonishment from behind the desk; but the origin of the whistle was unseen: the man was hidden completely behind the wall of cans and bottles and packages.

The man got up and walked around to the front of the desk.

"You got the money to pay for all this?"

Obediently, Farley emptied his pockets of all the money he had left—nearly thirty dollars.

"Not enough," the voice came.

Suddenly the other spoke, very rapidly, excited: "I been watching you. You thought you was pretty smart, but we of Murcherson's know a thing or two too. We ain't asleep on our feet, are we, Mr. Dahl?"

"Arrest me," Farley said.

"*I'll bet he's a pervert*," the pale face said.

But the other ignored him. "Too much trouble to prosecute. Lucky you got this money. When he gets here, Mr. Murcherson'll talk to you; he likes to talk to you people; then I see you so much as a mile from here I kick your ass from hell to back."

"I would like to be arrested," Farley said.

"Why?" the man asked.

"I'm evil."

But then his eyes went to the high ceiling again; the room spun down on him; he fainted.

When he awoke, four hands were dragging him toward a door: it opened: a light down some deep hole went on, blazing. Between them, upright, he was dragged down the wooden steps: smells of rotting garbage; another door, heavily locked. On his feet in the middle of the room, he shivered from the cold: beyond the locked door was the street. He staggered against a can overflowing with rotten vegetables: a huge white rat darted from behind it, clattering others. He heard the steps ascended; the door slammed heavily shut; the light went off, leaving him in darkness.

He stood very still for a long time; he listened. At last he heard sounds: sharp claws scratching the concrete floor; something burrowing noisily among trash. Again there was the frantic scratching; then a squeak; another. He knew he must not move; he must not fall to that concrete floor; but every nerve in him screamed to rush up those stairs to the door.

Again he heard the squeakings; a can rattled: something burrowing among rot and slime. The quick scratching sounds came nearer: he could hear them converging from every part of the room; the squeakings grew more numerous, converging too. Another can rattled, a box toppled, sending the squeakings into hysterical chorus. One ran past him, almost cunning; another scurried above, not far from him, he thought, upon a rafter; two more shot past, one hitting a wall and skittering off, claws tearing; returned as if blind toward him, hitting his foot.

"MOMMA," he screamed.

Plunging blindly toward the stairs, stumbling against the wooden railing, he scrambled up them upon hands and knees. He rose to his feet; fell; got upright again; lunged into the door and pounded upon it

"I won't do it again," he was screaming. *"I promise I won't do it again!"*

He could hear the skitterings and squeakings behind him now: in clusters, they scrambled upon the steps toward him. One hit his shoe again; another clambered over it. He was screaming and pounding still when one flew, as if from some niche or rafter, onto his shoulder, claws digging to maintain balance, then thudding off.

Farley fell after it, tumbling and spinning among them upon the stairs and landing upon the concrete floor where he lay screaming for mother, for God, for anything.

8

For weeks Lenore had been preparing for her trip. Where she was going she did not know. But it was always like that: some intuition told her that what had been was nearly finished; some circumference of dream was diminishing, and another lay somewhere on that road that would begin. And so she had started her peculiar but, to her, very necessary preparations.

She had $14.65; that was enough. She even felt very rich in the possession of it, and since she distrusted the value of paper money, she had taken the bills to one of the bars and exchanged them for coins. These she had spent days shining; they glistened now, each stacked in piles according to their denominations, in a cigar box at the bottom of one of her cartons of clothes.

The next thing was the clothes: she had to select a wardrobe, and this was always a problem to her. She had no idea what clothes were proper to be worn anywhere; she might recognize one as a tennis outfit, and yet it seemed somehow to her that it should be worn at a party, or to have dinner in; and so for hours she sat sorting out the various articles of clothing, selecting and rejecting and selecting again and again; only to repeat the process, not with confusion, or even anger at her impotence, but always curiously, questioningly, as if expecting to find among them some elusive but marvelous revelation of their true character and meaning. She was not in a hurry; she would be prepared when the time came.

And it was not a dull time either; these never were for her: she used it to record finally the meaning of the house, and the people in it. This was necessary in order that she might store it away with the other houses, the other people—a by now sizable collection that she kept exactly recorded that she might, whenever she felt the need, bring it forth to amuse herself, or puzzle over, during periods of loneliness or depression.

The device she used to achieve this recording of the lives of people she had known was a very simple one, and one she had never revealed to anyone: she could register instantaneously, store, and call forth even years later entire conversations she had heard. Her genius for mimicry would have seemed astounding had she ever revealed it to anyone: she could bring from herself the exact voices, intonations and word-for-word recall of any conversation she overheard; but of course this was a secret thing, as were her conversations with the Father-God. She had never even considered revealing it to anyone, even the young, bearded boy who had gone off.

For months this talent had been unused; she had become plunged so far into the darkness of the world that had surrounded Farley that it had frightened her even to attempt it: she had no need to record what she knew clearly was a raging but incomplete madness. But now she knew the trip was imminent; she was preparing for another beginning; and during that last week she had begun, as a tourist might photograph the scenes he was visiting for inclusion in his album, to record the voices and conversations, and even the gestures, of those in the house.

Now, tired from the day's activities of sorting the clothes and counting and arranging the coins again, she would relax after that day's work by listening in on the conversations that took place in the house; and when Farley had come in reeling, sick and bruised, when she had seen how fast the fever raged and started tending him in her own clumsy but determined way, she had been brought into closer contact with those people who now roamed over all the house. She had recorded some while tending Farley, others while hidden away and listening in secret places she knew.

In the evenings she would relax with them; she would close her door and re-create them. It was a private and very wonderful time for her: here her world was ordered as a tape is edited: she could excise for the moment any part that was disagreeable or disturbing to her; and yet it would be exact; it would be a world she had captured from others.

She would mimic the voices of the people who now

lived in the house: even her features and posture would change to approximate them. She would walk across the room, cheeks inflated and feet pounding heavily in the lumbering walk of one of the fat whores: her voice would be harsh and whiskey-hollow as she brought forth the, to her, funny obscenities of the woman; or she would be one of the twisted beggars (she would drag painfully across the room for this) whining his woes to a neighbor; the dwarf with his high, excited gibberings; or the Prophet himself, reeling drunk and berating the others. She preferred the comic ones, of course; she could make play with them. Now and then, as in an old-style movie, she would introduce a villain; but more often she would do the comic ones, those to her that *became* comic anyway, removed from their actual flesh.

Now too she did Farley; and that was the strange part: there was no more Farley. At least, that boy she had first known at the party in Bolinas had gone; she could not doubt that when she brought forth his voice and speeches and gestures: he was gone; and what had replaced him was some nebulous, unfinished thing, some thing, in fact, that so frightened her that she had not re-created him very often. As she had tended him during those four days of hysteria and fever on his mattress, she recorded his utterings: they were dark and full of fear of wild things she knew must rear inside of him: there was no trace of the boy-Farley she had first known—the intense but comic one, the Gentleman Caller. He had gone; and not in the way that Thorn and the young bearded boy had gone; gone strangely and incompletely while still present in body. For that reason, she did not do Farley often; she had put him away for some other time when she might better understand him.

But she *had* watched him. When at last he was well and the fever was gone, he had gotten fully dressed: clean suit and shirt and tie; but he had only gone out for a while and then returned; when he had, it was as if he had seen something startling out there, and had hurried back to the house to retreat from it. After that, each morning, he would be fully dressed, as if preparing to take a journey himself; but he never went; he seldom even left the room. He would sit upon the one chair in the room, against the wall, or upon the edge of the mattress, and he would hardly move. He appeared inhuman to her then; his face was expressionless. He seemed to be waiting for something.

This, she was convinced, was a sort of activity: it was part of some obscure rite he was performing; and when after days of this the other things began, she was more puzzled than ever.

At first it was the pieces of glass: he had broken some of the beer bottles into many pieces; these he had strewn on the floor of the room. And then, fully dressed still except for shoes and socks, he had walked back and forth upon them for periods of time. She had looked on wincing: she could see the bloodied imprints of his footsteps each time he came off the path of glass. When he was done, he would wash his feet, put on his shoes and socks, and return to his sitting, as if having performed for that day his necessary labors. Another time she had followed him onto the roof, looking through a crack in the door at him during one of the coldest days. He had stood a few minutes looking out over the gray sheet-like sky: a few clouds hung limp as dishrags in it; and then slowly, piece by piece, placing them neatly upon his lion's-paw chair, he had taken off his clothes and stood naked there, shivering, for a long time. There were other things too: once he had hung himself for nearly all of one night by the wrists, tying the rope to the inside of the doorknob of his closet and placing a chair just in reach of him; another time he had taken his carving knife from under the mattress where he now kept it and, sharpening it upon a piece of stone for nearly an hour, had lay on the mattress and there made small, deft incisions into his skin, blood rising upon each one.

But she had finally fled these scenes; she preferred the others.

Each day she would steal out to some secret place where she might record them further.

At the moment of dawn, Farley arose from the mattress. To someone who watched, it might seem he had lain there for hours, eyes open and awaiting the light, for there was no trace of the derangement of sleep. He was fully clothed; his suit was unwrinkled, as if not slept in at all. At night now he lay stretched out full length on the mattress, his arms rigid at his sides; at first light, he arose.

Hurriedly, almost as if the act were distasteful to him, and a waste of precious time, he gulped down part of a loaf of bread that had lain wrapped in newspaper beside the mattress; then he sat down on the chair to wait.

He began again to arrange his thoughts of the days of his illness and fever. He remembered Lenore vaguely; he supposed she must have brought him food and looked after him: no one else had appeared during that time. It was as if that illness had walled him off further from the others: they feared it, and would not confront it.

The times he had gone through the rooms, he had seen that they were inundated now: the derelicts were everywhere. In the front room perhaps twenty of them sat over various children's games. It was early winter; a harsh wind rattled the flimsy window even now; and they leaned heavy in grayness, the games their only occupation. A few looked glassy-eyed, insensate from them, as if having played at them ceaselessly for days on end; others slept finally as if drugged, half-finished games before them. Perhaps the Monopoly set he had stolen had started them; whatever the reason, they were absorbed only in those games now: Bingo and Scrabble and Ships and Tiddly Winks and Pick-Up Sticks and Chinese Checkers and Authors. Almost certainly they had stolen these; they could hardly have acquired them any other way.

He knew they were there, and that is why he did not go often through the rooms; they were everywhere, and instinctively he feared them.

In the sunless winter now they had come as if by scent; they possessed the rooms.

Already one or two had entered his room; he saw signs: little bits of casually discarded food; things disarranged with feeble cunning; and once (With what jubilant, sly smiles had it been done?), one small, miserly turd deposited like a calling card in the middle of his mattress.

The front room was a shambles: a hole had been punched in one of the pasteboard walls; a large and artlessly obscene drawing in crayon across one wall of a man and a woman in curiously laconic coitus. Like children, in their boredom they were waiting out the long winter; and like children, boredom was insufferable.

And so they bent, each one of them, hour upon hour, over the children's games; they waited; and Farley waited with them.

During those days in the chair, there was an image that Farley had been trying to bring into focus; now, with that progression, it was assuming clarity: it was that perhaps there was not one beast, but many that formed the one; that it drew apart and merged again and again, as the cells in a human organism. But in this, each was complete in itself; each could merge at will into the enormous whole: they could, one day, be that towering thing that would come at last to devour him. . . . Now he saw them singly; dozens upon dozens of them coming and going, in every corner of the rooms; finally they would unite. If he were quiet, it would not be soon; and so he sat each day in his chair silent.

That morning it began.

Suddenly the door was flung open and the Prophet stood in it, swaying. He was drunk (he was always drunk now); behind him, two small, grinning men. Those tiny eyes fierce, he lunged toward Farley; his hand went out, smashing him to the floor.

"*Mother, I want whiskey,*" he shouted. "Go get me some, you hear? You don't do nothing around here no more."

He turned and was gone.

A moment later, Farley went past the snickering faces into the street.

The street was the worst: it frightened him more than the house; for in the house at least the thing was contained; he knew its presence and movements; but here it might come from anywhere. He went slowly, hugging the walls of buildings; he took long moments at corners, not daring to cross until no car was in sight, for if one was even blocks away he knew it would speed up suddenly with cruel cunning, catching him there and running him over. It was the kind of hysteria he knew he must keep firmly controlled: if once let loose, he might be devoured by it. He walked then cautiously, upon the periphery of objects; to passersby, it appeared he was lurching. Each object was a threat; each at any moment might become animate and attack him.

It was an hour later when he approached a market where he knew he might get the whiskey; but he knew even then it was useless, and as he stood before the long shelves, he could only look; he was frozen; and he had turned quickly and run from the place back to the house, past the now-laughing faces. The Prophet sat there grinning, a full bottle of whiskey beside him.

That night there seemed to be some sort of party in the house: there was yelling and someone was playing a harmonica; loud drunken voices and dancing. Again the door was flung open; again the Prophet stood in it, blacker and more immense in the half-light.

This time he did not speak at all: he strode to Farley and, one hand encircling his neck, dragged him, as one would a kitten, into the front room, where the others sat and lay, as if eagerly awaiting a show.

The Prophet threw Farley into the middle of the floor and sat down on his mattress with a bottle. A little man with a screwed-up face like a monkey held the harmonica to his mouth waiting happily; at a signal from the Prophet, he began to play.

"Dance," the Prophet said.

Farley danced.

After that he was not left alone for a moment: they were always at him. At first it was just the Prophet:

Farley's fall had made him his personal victim. But, discarding their games now, soon the others began to join in. It was like a dance—some weird, chthonian dance in which each one used him in his turn, and then passed him on to another. Day and night Farley awaited these calls. He would be sent on trivial errands for the Prophet; he would be made to cook and serve meals as each required; and in the evenings, he would be brought in for their entertainment in some game or new diversion they had devised.

Farley would lie on his mattress; he would hear footsteps. After a moment, the door would open and one of the grinning, twisted faces, nearly disembodied in the half-light of the hallway, would peer in at him: a finger would be crooked at him, beckoning, and he would get up wearily and go into them. Or, asleep for a moment upon his mattress, he would jerk suddenly awake to see them standing around looking down at him and whispering; or in darkness, one would pounce upon him in sleep and run off giggling. Now Farley would return to find his clothes strewn about the floor, or hidden away from him; he would open his closet upon the stench of excrement and urine deposited there during his absence. While some slept, others used him; and when these tired, there were always others still.

One night, the Prophet called him.

As he stood waiting in the front room, he heard first giggles; then huge laughter; and as he finally looked up, he saw the Prophet holding out at him, one in each hand, the heart-shaped woman's panties and long, golden wig.

"Look what *we* found," he said. "Gertrude," he added.

They *howled* with laughter, the dwarf rolling upon the floor and beating his chest.

Farley looked up then in sick entreaty: he tried to call forth from him the love and tenderness he thought once he had shared with the giant: there was none; only that cold, mocking face with the curious eyes imbedded deep in it. Farley's torture was immense: he had been betrayed; worse, *revealed*; and he hated him then.

"Strip," the Prophet said.

In a moment Farley stood naked before them all. Someone shrieked with laughter beside him; one of the drunken whores: her voice rose like a bird gone mad. She lay arms and legs flung out, naked except for panties and brassiere.

The Prophet saw the leopard then; he could not have missed it; and what had been once a declaration of love Farley knew now would serve his rage further: the eyes studied him contemptuously. The others had seen it too: they came now in awe to him to peer closely at it. Several touched it; then they scampered away as the Prophet threw the panties and wig onto the floor before Farley.

"Put 'em on, mother," he said.

Farley got into the panties and wig. He stood shivering.

"Dance now, white boy."

The harmonica began with a little jerking sound, like something unwinding, and as they watched, Farley danced. It was a very quiet, somber dance, and even their faces reflected it.

Suddenly the Prophet stood up, lurching. Staggering so that he almost fell, he lunged toward Farley. He took Farley's hands and, leading, the golden curls bouncing upon the wig on Farley's head, danced him in long, jumping strides around the room.

In panic, Farley drew in his stomach; his legs bent back.

Round and around they danced until Farley could see the room whirling; faces and bodies and furniture spun past.

At its heighth, when he felt he could no longer stand, Farley was flung off. He seemed to whirl, tumbling, in space; the faces and bodies flew past him; and he found himself sprawled out across the drunken, leering whore.

Farley scrambled to get to his feet, but in his dizziness he could not rise. Already two bony arms were around him; the drunken face was breathing into his as he felt himself being wrenched slowly and interminably down.

When he just lay there, panting, the others began to laugh. Slowly, the room came back into focus: the faces were all leaning over him, waiting; and then the whore threw him off with a curse of contempt, and he found himself crawling back to his room amid derisive laughter.

They were moving him at night: for the past five nights this had been their newest game. Now they would let Farley sleep. Exhausted, he would plunge hungrily into blackness. Dreams would jerk him up now and then; arms and legs would flail out in sleep, body rear up in spasms; then he would sink into blackness again . . . until they came.

Sometimes Farley would hear the door creak open slowly; sometimes not. Sometimes he would not even be aware of how long they had been standing there in the darkness around him. But sooner or later he would feel hands reach out of the darkness to grab him: they would encircle him; then he would be lifted up.

He never cried out; not once did he resist. In a moment he would be borne by them from the room through the darkened other rooms. Always he knew that none slept. He would hear a foot scrape; someone would giggle, and be shushed; once his bearers nearly stumbled over one in the darkness. He could *feel* them there, awake and watching his progress, some perhaps even following, through the rooms. There seemed to be no hurry about it; it was processional; and he imagined an escort surrounding him too, bearing invisible flambeaux. . . . Finally, they would lower him to his destination; he would feel the cold floor beneath him; and he would plunge again as quickly as possible into sleep.

So he had no room of his own now; he had only where they selected him to be each night. Once it was the bathroom; another time, beneath the kitchen table. In the morning, they watched as he awoke; they looked on happily to see his surprise; and when he crawled back at last to his own room, he would find one of them upon his mattress. Then he would await the day of games and taunts to begin again.

There is a contagion of abuse upon published victims. It is as if a scent goes out from them; some look of the eye perhaps that signifies. When this is known, each will come to take his turn; feed themselves upon the victim.

Now Farley signalled that condition to all: he felt he could not go upon the street without some scorn or abuse hurled at him. That scent preceded him; it announced his coming: all were aware that a prey was at large.

The Prophet would send him on an errand, and he would watch person after person waited on in the store before him; clerks spoke to him shortly and with scorn; policemen bullied him back onto sidewalks while other pedestrians went unmolested.

Farley would walk then nearly imbedded into the sides of buildings; he avoided crowds for fear of them suddenly recognizing him and turning upon him and beating him.

He was alone . . . he was the hunted.

When they had at last become bored with the game of moving him at night, they began other games. It was now as if no moment of the day or night was his. He was not allowed to sleep; he could hardly eat for fear they had done something to his food; and there was no such thing as avoiding their always-watching eyes. He suspected guards were assigned to him when he was sent on an errand: each beggar or cripple he saw was his possible captor.

Not even the girl's room seemed sacred now, although until then they had not molested her. Several times he had gone to her room as refuge. Once he thought he heard voices in the room, and he had stood still in the hallway for minutes listening, afraid they were there too; but when the voices stopped suddenly, and he entered, he saw she was alone in the middle of the floor, nearly hidden by the long black dress and sorting out the clothes. But even so, he knew they were watching.

The furniture began to go: first little things here and there; then one day the two couches were gone; and then other things: when he looked one day, nearly all of his clothes; and upon each disappearance, food and bottles appeared to take their place. Within a week it was nearly all gone. It was, to Farley, like a slow, trick movie: day by day the rooms became more naked and harsh; in time, there would be only the rooms themselves, a final wilderness.

Now too there was filth everywhere; stink and rot

as in that cellar. The toilet was broken and clogged with mess; piles of excrement in every room; the sinks and floors smelled always of urine; and he had to stumble through places where the discarded food cartons and bottles and remains of meals were piled high. He could see them rising; he could see himself engulfed in them, smothering at last beneath a mountain of stink and debris.

The Prophet no longer sent him on errands; he had designated him worthless now for any but the most menial chores; and so night and day he was called out to prepare food or clear spaces in the front room that they might continue their parties.

Now couples lay entangled; he could hear them straining and see them writhing upon the floor; and when they at last disengaged, became two again, they would look up with drunken, glazed eyes at him, upon hands and knees, as if about to pounce. Sometimes, one of these would be the Prophet, and Farley would be sick as he was forced to look on: the great black body would pound; as it rose and fell, Farley's gasps would rise and fall with it; it would pulse and thrust, the nearly hidden white body writhing too beneath it. Farley would flee the room.

One night the Prophet had him stand naked again before them all. Farley was very thin now: his bony arms and legs stuck out awkwardly; and now there was no heat in the apartment (the rent had not been paid in months) and Farley stood shivering before them. He did not really mind the nakedness: it was not the first time, and he was almost inured to their snickerings and leers; but now he knew, he *had* known for weeks, that he was hardly any longer even a man.

When they saw him this time, they *all* laughed. The little dwarf came out to inspect him: coming barely to its level, he stared curiously, almost in awe.

"You ain't no man *atall*," the Prophet pronounced from his mattress, and they all laughed.

"If you ain't no man then," the Prophet said, "be a dog."

When Farley looked up questioningly at him, the Prophet had already risen and taken Farley by the neck and forced him onto all fours. Farley watched as the rope he had used to hang himself from his door was produced; with a noose tied in it, it was dropped over his head like a leash. Then he was led around the room by the dwarf.

When the Prophet told him to bark, he barked; then he was led round again.

Finally released, he fled to a corner of the kitchen beneath the sink, which was his only refuge now; but later he was called to repeat the performance; and again; and then whenever he tried to sleep, had slunk off to his spot beneath the sink, he would find the dwarf straddling him like a jockey. The dwarf would beat his buttocks with his tiny hands and Farley would rise wearily and amble off with him.

Winter had come; it slashed the windows; and in the unheated apartment, even the taunting of Farley lacked now the inventiveness they had displayed before, although there was still no peace for him.

They sat bent and sullen in the big rooms: their grayness matched that of the beaten sky outside the windows; and now they began to fight among themselves.

Farley would watch, crouched, from behind a doorway or corner. During the day, he would see them tumbling endlessly, soundlessly, rolling back and forth across the floor—as if even the energy required to give voice to their anger could not be summoned. But at night, after they had turned off the lights, it was worse; then he could only hear them: little groanings and wheezings; wordless; like animals in silent, fierce combat.

That night the moon shone brightly; three-quarters full and pale orange. The sky was as black as the satin dress the girl wore: upright, feathery clouds flew across the moon like a flight of geese, but slowly.

Farley sat in darkness upon the kitchen floor looking out the window at that nightsky; it drew him. He thought for some minutes about how he might open the window and glide up, sucked into the blackness; to whirl, perhaps, safely forever in space. He could hear the others behind him; in a moment one of them would come for him he knew: it would slink in the darkness behind him and carry him off; they would claw over him again.

He could not remember now very clearly how he

had gotten there among them; he knew only that there did not seem to be any end to them.

Now he could hear the Prophet bellowing in the front room; a bottle smashed against a wall. He knew the reason: he could smell the heat in the man.

For days the giant had come to abuse him about what they had all seen in the room when he was naked. How could he have a woman, and be like that? He was no man; he had shown he could be a dog; what good was she to him?

Farley refused to answer. He had just cringed, morose, in his corner beneath the sink. Now Farley could hear them laughing in there: there was some new game planned; they had been nearly all the day at it. But he shut his mind to that. . . .

The moon was so clean and beautiful he nearly leaned up to grasp it; a sound of awe went up from him. If he kept very still, he thought, and looked and thought only of the moon, he might not feel the presence of the others. As it was, they seemed to slither into him on paths of darkness: where the darkness was, they came to life and reached out for him.

Then they came for him.

In the center of the room the dwarf stood, grinning. It was as if a scene in a play had been prepared for him with great care, and now he was ushered in at its curtain, its sole audience.

The dwarf wore a cardboard-and-paper facsimile of a tuxedo, or evening suit. It was crudely done, and colored with crayons from one of the games. The tiny man wore a black top hat made from cardboard; the shirt front was cardboard too, colored white, with a black evening tie drawn upon it; the white dress gloves were made by cutting and pasting pieces of colored paper together; even the flower pinned to his lapel was of tissue paper. He looked strange there; unreal; for he dared not move in his flimsy dress: a knee thrust up would rip the pinned paper trousers; a movement of his arm would send the elbow tearing into the cardboard coat; he was imprisoned. But uncomfortable as he apparently was, he still grinned.

Farley was led to him and made to stand beside him. The little man craned his neck and looked with amusement and, perhaps, even affection up at him.

The Prophet was standing before them, a black book in one hand, and he too had been dressed in paper: a preacher. But although unmoving in the flimsy raiment (even the round black hat of a preacher), Farley knew that he might not stay contained; there was about him the threat of at any moment ripping out of it.

The Prophet was facing Farley, as in a wedding ceremony; flanking him, two of the old whores, as twisted and thin as twin grasshoppers, stood holding paper baskets filled nearly to overflowing with twisted flowers of colored tissue paper.

Behind him, Farley could see, two of the winos had mounted the windowsill and were taking down Farley's drapes; behind these were the lace curtains he had not seen once since coming to the house. Now they had gotten to the floor and were approaching Farley with them from behind.

The Prophet did not move; he could not have without tearing his mock clothes; but at a signal to the two behind with his eyes, Farley felt the golden wig fitted to his head; the lace curtains followed, two hands at his sides and bringing them over his head and shoulders and chest, where they fell to the floor like a long wedding veil. Another signal from the Prophet, and then he felt the dwarf reach up and place his small hand in his.

The Prophet began, reading from the book: "Dearly beloved, we are gathered here in the presence of these witnesses to unite this man and this woman in holy wedlock."

The Prophet paused only a few seconds; he would have gone on, but, in his drunkenness, faltered; and that was when, in the unexpected silence, all of them heard the second voice, clearly and in exactly the voice of the Prophet:

"Dearly beloved, we are gathered here . . ."

Instantly the Prophet turned, catching a glimpse of the enraptured face of Lenore from the hallway corner: his elbow came through the torn sleeve of his paper coat; and just as quickly, her face was withdrawn. In the silence that followed they all heard the soft but quick footsteps back to the room.

It took a moment longer: the Prophet could not grasp the truth of what had happened too quickly; but when at last he did, he straightened, as if blown up more immense still.

"NAWWWWW," he screamed, and in horror Farley watched as he ripped out of his false suit, shed it crumbling around him in fistfuls: it was as if he were shedding another, brittle skin; and when he was free, when the debris of it lay scattered over all of them, he reached out and picked up Farley by the shoulders, lifted him at first high above his head, and then hurled him at the wall, the wig and lace curtains flying off behind.

Farley lost consciousness for only a minute: the mattress he fell on had saved him; but when he looked up and started to get to his knees he saw that the Prophet had now shed his real clothes too. The dwarf then, until that moment stone-still in fear, burst suddenly from his paper clothes, trampling pieces of them underfoot in his haste; and then they moved out of the room in the direction in which Lenore had fled.

When Farley got to the door, they were crammed into the room. It was as if they had all come out and converged at last from every corner and hiding place in the rooms: the room was packed with the twitching creatures. He could see Lenore clearly only for moments at a time, crouched against one wall, eyes wider still in horror. Beside her, one of the whores had taken the lace curtains and draped them over the trembling girl's shoulders; another fitted them to her head. Finished, they moved off, and two more came forward with their baskets of flowers. They cleared a space for a moment before the wide-eyed girl; then they began a little grotesque dance before her, strewing handfuls of the fake flowers over her.

The next moment, though, Farley could see the Prophet's figure lunging in the room. It appeared and disappeared; stooping, then standing to his full height, he brought up with him each time one of the derelicts: as if gone mad and destroying a mannequin workshop. Now one of the derelicts would fly off against a wall; another would be sent hurtling into the tightly gathered people, rushing them to the floor in a confusion of bodies; and sudden panic in all the others.

"Get out mothers, white mothers," at last the Prophet roared; and those who could rushed past Farley down the hall; and as the giant lunged forward, gathering them with him to the door like a wave, others broke loose and ran, one sending Farley to the floor.

Then there was the noise of the Prophet grunting in his labors; the sounds of flesh pounded by those massive fists, and Farley, hugging the wall, was stamped and fallen upon in the rush of bodies; and only after the Prophet had passed were they all gone, driven before him, from the rooms.

He heard the door shut; lock; then, Farley's head buried in his arms, he heard the Prophet stomping and mumbling as he moved in the narrow, dark hallway toward him. Farley lay still; he expected at any moment to feel the fists club down upon him; but whether in drunkenness and the semi-darkness of the hallway

188

he did not see, or whether Farley was now so far degraded that his presence did not matter, he passed by; the door closed.

Then the sounds came.

At first Farley could not recognize them; and then, strangely, he heard something of his own voice in them; and then the Prophet's too: each clearly for a moment, unmistakable, and then diminishing, to be drowned out by the other; and then other, faintly familiar voices; but hysterically, a quick procession of now-familiar, now-unknown voices and conversations; then there were no voices that he knew; they were all unknown. Precisely then, with almost horrible speed, they ran on; more and more quickly until garbled; until for seconds one voice would blend into others, others would rise to dominate that one, and then be lost beneath the sea of more dominant voices still; and then finally so quickly, so hysterically, there were no voices at all, just a great screeching sound in which there were only fleeing hints of them; like a tape run at mad speed; faster still; until at last that tape ran out; there were no voices; just a great void of sudden, spinning silence.

Farley waited a moment in that silence, then got to his feet; he made his way creeping to his room. Even in darkness, he found his carving knife in seconds beneath the mattress; he held it to his chest like a sacrament a moment; then listening, still cautiously, he began to move out of the room and back down the hall.

He knew that if he went too quickly, if he stumbled or made some noise, all would be lost; but if he went quickly and silently both while it was still distracted, he might succeed. Crouched over to be as unobtrusive as possible, he moved to the door and opened it a crack.

A giant mouth seemed to be feeding there: upon the bed, a white, small form was being devoured by it: only the arms and legs rooted out of the mouth, the legs kicking up uselessly, but the arms pounding and tearing at it.

Farley stood, eyes wide, gaping.

When he moved into the room, he was more cautious still; he was trembling before it; but he closed his mind to it, and when he drew closer, the mouth seemed to move even more hungrily: it opened and closed rapidly upon the struggling form upon the bed.

Then, quietly, he stood above it; he brought the knife up as high as he could reach; and then down swiftly into the blackness.

The thing convulsed; it bucked up, the knife still imbedded. One black arm appeared, fingers searching frantically for the buried hilt; but in a second, before they could reach it, Farley had pulled the knife smoothly out and the creature had rolled over onto the bed.

For a second, Farley saw the whiteness of the released girl roll from the bed; but only for a second; for then *it* began to move up. It had beady eyes now wide with horror and disbelief. Slowly it began to rise, and

Farley raised the knife high again, leaned forward and brought it down just under the chest.

It quivered a moment; a pool of blood grew now richly red on its blackness; then its eyes opened wider still in disbelief; it shuddered and fell back.

The turban was off; it lay beside the still figure.

Farley withdrew the knife and put it beside the body; then the turban; then he drew the lavender sheet around it. He went out of the room and into the front room where his rope with the noose still in it lay where it had been discarded; with this, he returned to the room, tying it around the sheet so it would not fall away.

It took perhaps twenty minutes for Farley to drag it to the roof. There he untied the rope and loosened the sheet around the form. He slipped the noose under the arms, still holding the sheet around it, pushed it up onto the edge of the roof and slowly, supporting the rope against the ledge, lowered it.

Farley could see it receding toward the ground; dangling, now and then bumping against the wall and spinning slightly; but when the rope was played out, the body was still one story from the ground, and he let go and heard it thud onto the courtyard below.

Then Farley went down into the kitchen and found a large cooking spoon and went out of the house, over the door and into the courtyard.

He climbed the piked fence to the space between it and the small statue of Christ.

It took nearly three hours before he was through,

but he was not in the least tired; he was alive with energy. For the first time he could feel the real, hidden strength of righteousness surging in him; he hummed to himself the "Hallelujah Chorus" as he dug.

But when at last it was finished and he had dragged and pushed the body over it into the hole, he saw that it would not fit in the small space allowed by the fence. So he opened the sheet, took out the knife and spent most of the rest of the night hacking off both legs and buried them with him before the white Christ.

At the actual moment of entombment, however, when the last clod of dirt had been placed over the grave, the moon that had been so bright to him that night dimmed: upon his knees, Farley looked up and saw a filmy cloud covering it. A moment later another, denser cloud slid over it, and he was in shadows; and then he was in darkness.